Doctor Thomas Neill Cream

Doctor Thomas Neill Cream: Mystery at McGill

David Fennario

Talonbooks   Vancouver   1993

Published with the assistance of the Canada Council

Talonbooks
201 - 1019 East Cordova
Vancouver, British Columbia
Canada V6A 1M8

Typeset in New Baskerville by Pièce de Résistance Ltée., and printed and bound in Canada by Hignell Printing Ltd.

First Printing: November 1993

Rights to produce *Doctor Thomas Neill Cream (Mystery at McGill)*, in whole or in part, in any medium, by any group, amateur or professional, are retained by the author. Interested persons should apply to him c/o Talonbooks, #201 - 1019 East Cordova, Vancouver, B.C., Canada, V6A 1M8.

Music scores executed by Waylen Miki

Canadian Cataloguing in Publication Data

Fennario, David, 1947-
        Doctor Thomas Neill Cream (mystery at McGill)

        A play.
        ISBN 0-88922-332-7

        I. Title.
PS8561.E54D6 1993   C812'.54   C93-091779-0
PR9199.3.F45D6 1993

pour Jean Yves

PRODUCTION CREDITS

Doctor Thomas Neill Cream (Mystery at McGill) premiered on November 2, 1988, at Mixed Company, Toronto, with the following cast:

LADY ALLAN..Kathryn Boese
SIR HUGH ALLAN...Allen Booth
SIR WILLIAM OSLER..Mark Christmann
LEPINE/REVOLUTIONARY....................................Jennifer Dean
NATI MASCOU..Leanne Haze
DARLINGTON/REVOLUTIONARY......................Merle Matheson
CAMILLE...Diane Pitblado
LORD STRATHCONA...Michael Polley
DOCTOR THOMAS NEILL CREAM.......................Julian Richings
SIR WILFRID LAURIER...Pierre Tetrault

Directed by Simon Malbogat
Music by Allen Booth
Set Realization by Jacqueline Fine
Set Painting by Elizabeth Asselstine & Jacqueline Fine
Lighting by Mary Wright
Costumes by Audrey Vanderstoop
Costume Maintenance by April Hubert
Props by Leslie Lester
Stage Manager: Micheline Chevrier
Assistant Stage Manager: Neil Scott
Funhouse Display by Sheila Salmela

SET AND STAGING

The style of the play is presentational and operatic. The story of Cream is presented in a narrative fashion that shifts in time and place. Often the characters are there doing the story, but usually they are telling the story as they remember it. The actions in the play are not always acted out. They are presented in a courtroom fashion. This is what was done. This is what we saw. This is what we felt. Do you believe it?

THE DEAD, as a chorus and in character, attempt to defend themselves as historic figures. THE WOMEN as a chorus and in character, want revenge. CREAM, the murderer, wants the audience to know that the "Illustrious Dead" of McGill were no better than himself.

The play can be done with a cast of nine, doing multiple roles, or with a larger cast.

§

A sign at the front entry welcomes the audience to an exhibition entitled "McGill University: The First Hundred Years," honouring some of the benefactors and illustrious alumni of McGill University in Montreal.

Central to the theatre-in-the-round set is the tomb of James McGill. Attached to the four audience sections are displays celebrating the careers and achievements of LORD STRATHCONA of the Strathcona Hall of Anatomy, SIR WILLIAM OSLER of the Osler Library, SIR HUGH ALLAN of the Allan Memorial Hospital, and SIR WILFRID LAURIER of the Laurier Hall.

The James McGill display provides an illustration of McGill along with a biography. Other parts of the display consists of gloves, a cane, a top hat and a portrait of Sir

John Colborne, the British General who crushed the Rebellion of 1837-38. On top of the tomb are two decorative feminine figures in hooded robes in positions of lamentation.

The Sir Wilfrid Laurier display has a portrait of Laurier and a biography. Included as artifacts: a gold ring, photographs of Laurier as a young man, of his wife, and of his mistress. By pushing a button, audience members can light up a supposed wax figure representing Sir Wilfrid Laurier behind a scrim screen.

The Lord Dufferin display has a portrait of Lord Dufferin and a biography. Included as artifacts are souvenirs of his official visits as Governor General to Montreal. By pushing a button, audience members can light up a supposed wax figure representing Lord Dufferin behind a scrim screen.

The Sir Hugh Allan display provides a portrait of Allan and a biography. Included among the artifacts is a copy of the lithograph from the *Canadian Illustrated Magazine*, November 1872, depicting the welcoming of Lord Dufferin, the British Governor General of Canada, by Sir Hugh Allan to his house. By pushing a button, audience members can light up a supposed wax figure representing Sir Hugh Allan, behind a scrim screen.

The Lord Strathcona display has a portrait of Strathcona along with a biography. Other illustrations include a photo of the Nascapi people in Labrador, the famous shot of Strathcona hammering in "The Last Spike," and one of his mansion on Dorchester Street. Also on display, a necklace of caribou teeth and a railway spike—replica of "The Last Spike." By pushing a button, audience members can light up a supposed wax figure representing Lord Strathcona behind a scrim screen.

The Sir William Osler display provides a portrait and a biography of Osler. It has early photographs of medical students at McGill, along with the graduation picture of Thomas Neill Cream's class. Also included: a skull; a glass bell jar containing a stomach, liver and kidney pickled in formaldehyde; and a glass bottle labelled "Chloroform." By pushing a button, audience members can light up a supposed wax figure representing Osler behind a scrim screen.

The audience members, on their way to their seats, tour the set as they would a museum. They sense that things are not what they appear to be, not what they seem. They are seeing a façade with sinister hints of hidden corruption and decay: spider webs, rust stains and mildew. Sound of an autumn wind and distant strains of organ music. The appearance of the androgynous tour guide, handing out programmes, sets the tone. Is it a man or a woman? We are not sure. Once the audience members have taken their seats the tour guide, standing close by James McGill's tomb, prepares to speak.

§

GUIDE

Ladies and gentlemen: Now that you have taken your seats, I will present you with some background information on the illustrious figures that are featured here as part of an exhibition on McGill, celebrating over one hundred and eighty years of its existence. We will begin with the centrepiece, James McGill. Born in Glasgow, 1744, emigrating to North America in the 1770s. Soon after his arrival in Montreal, McGill became a prominent member of the Beaver Club, organized by a group of fur traders who had amassed considerable wealth in their calling. *(sudden screaming of an animal in pain)* When he died, McGill willed his estate and a large sum of money to establish a university. He knew that without the torch of a free and liberal education, the land of promise to which he had come and from which he had received much, could not advance to what he believed to be its destined place of power and service in the world.

9

Beginning chords of "O Canada" played in discordant fashion.

GUIDE

Caring as James McGill did for the unity of our great country, it is not surprising to learn that his university also attracted others of different faiths and languages, including Sir Wilfrid Laurier who studied Law at McGill University. Prime Minister of Canada, 1896-1911, Sir Wilfrid's career was a lengthy one, tinged with romance, full of drama and deeply tangled in the issues of the day.

VOICE

Please, oh please, no!

GUIDE

Sir Wilfrid Laurier believed in British Law because the rights of any citizen, whether Anglophone or Francophone, were protected. In that sense McGill is proud of its British heritage and honours here Lord Dufferin of Ava, Governor General of Canada, who, in a speech here at McGill in 1873, reminded the students that they were the best and brightest of their generation, the hope of a whole nation.

VOICE

Dead, all dead.

GUIDE

During one of his visits to Montreal, Lord Dufferin dined at Ravenscrag, the home of Sir Hugh Allan, a shipping magnate, railway promoter and financier. Later, the Allan family would donate their house to McGill University, with the understanding that whatever humanitarian use might be made of Ravenscrag, it would continue to be called "The Allan Memorial."

VOICE

Remember.

10

GUIDE

A contemporary of Sir Hugh Allan and one who helped McGill University become internationally known in medicine was Lord Strathcona, Governor of the Hudson's Bay Company, President of the Bank of Montreal, one of the financiers of the Canadian Pacific Railway, and Chancellor of McGill University.

VOICE

Lest We Forget.

GUIDE

Apart from countless gifts to individuals, Strathcona gave large sums to a few selected institutions, including sums for the establishment of the Royal Victorian College for Women and the Strathcona Hall of Anatomy.

VOICE

Don't let me do this thing!

GUIDE

And over here we have Sir William Osler, one of the great medical men, foremost pathologist and leading diagnostician of his time.

Sobbing sounds commence.

GUIDE

Osler attended McGill University where he became a teacher after graduation. As Chief Physician at the age of thirty-nine, he introduced revolutionary new techniques that have become standard practice throughout the world.

VOICE

I am not responsible for this!

GUIDE

Comrades and friends, on Remembrance Day here at McGill, we are gathered, not only to remember the Dead, but to honour them for their contributions to our school and to our nation. We pause in memory of the sacrifices they made in the past, so that we might prosper and benefit from their endeavors in the present. It can truly be said that those whom we celebrate here have indeed left their mark upon this institution. Can we not feel their presence as we look upon their work? Can we not hear their voices still in this place? The whispers and secrets, secrets and whispers, voices in the wind, in the rain, in the night, listen...

> *GUIDE fades out as light changes and autumn wind increases. Cawing of ravens leading into the voices heard in the wind. VOICES ONE to FOUR are feminine. VOICES FIVE to SEVEN are masculine.*

VOICE 4

Ravenscrag.

VOICE 6

Ravenscrag.

VOICE 5

Ravens—

VOICES 4, 5, 6

—crag

VOICE 4

Burning.

VOICE 6

Burning.

VOICES 5, 7

Burning.

VOICE 1

Wotshima.

VOICE 4

No, I said no.

VOICES 1, 2

Wotshima.

VOICES 4, 5

No.

VOICES 1, 2, 3

Wotshima.

VOICES 4, 5, 6, 7

No.

VOICES 1, 2, 3

O God of Bethel.

VOICES 4, 5, 6, 7

By Whose hand.

VOICE 2

Don't hurt me.

VOICES 4, 5

I only want to play with you.

VOICES 1, 2, 3

Don't hurt me.

VOICES 4, 5, 6, 7

I only want to play with you.

VOICE 1

Lies.

VOICES 2, 3

Lies.

13

                        VOICE 1
Lies.

                        VOICE 4
Camille.

                        VOICE 3
Am I going to die?

                        VOICES 4, 5
Camille.

                        VOICES 1, 2, 3
Am I going to die?

                        VOICES 4, 5, 6, 7
Lost.

                        VOICE 5
Lost.

                        VOICE 4
Let the Dead sleep.

                        VOICES 1, 2, 3
Remember.

                        VOICES 4, 5, 6, 7
Let the Dead sleep.

                        VOICES 1, 2, 3
Remember.

WOMEN ONE, TWO, THREE— who have been standing in place as ornamental figures on top of James McGill's tomb — have removed their robes and hoods, coming to life. They are dressed in dance hall costumes, their faces heavily rouged with spangled mascara that glitters.

14

WOMEN
(Singing to the tune of "Believe Me If All Those Endearing Young Charms")
Alma Mater McGill, we will sing to thy praise
From the Treasures of hearts fond and true
For the love in our hearts is awakened by thoughts
Which the prospects of parting renew
The friendships we've formed in thy halls are as dear
As the casket of memory holds
Time never can bring aught more tenderly sweet
As the Future its secrets unfolds.

WOMAN 2
McGill University.

WOMEN 1, 3
A place dedicated to science and education.

WOMAN 2
McGill University.

WOMEN 1, 3
One Hundred and Eighty Years of Progress.

WOMAN 2
McGill University.

WOMAN 1
"Beholding the Bright Countenance of Truth—

WOMAN 3
—in the Quiet and Still Air of Delightful Study."

WOMAN 2
McGill University.

WOMEN 1, 3
The people are dying.

15

WOMAN 2

The people are dying.

WOMEN 1, 3

(Holding up their right hands) Mort main.

WOMAN 2

Mort main.

WOMEN 1, 3

Mort main. *(The WOMEN lower their right hands.)*

The WOMEN lower their right hands.

WOMEN 1, 3

What the preachers will not preach.

WOMAN 2

What the teachers will not teach.

WOMEN 1, 3

McGill University.

WOMAN 2

There is murder in the city.

WOMEN 1, 3

Murder.

WOMAN 2

On November the eleventh, 1993, some workers excavating
a foundation for a new building on McGill campus,
discovered skeletal remains which were collected and
presented to the Strathcona Hall of Anatomy. The experts
agree that the remains were human but who they were or
how they died has remained a mystery, until tonight.

Strains of "Ravenscrag Rag" increasing in volume.

16

Calling Doctor Cream.

THE DEAD

We are alive in you.

WOMEN

Calling Doctor Cream.

THE DEAD

We are alive in you.

WOMEN

Calling Doctor Cream!

THE DEAD

Forever and ever.

WOMEN

He is getting stronger.

THE DEAD

Forever and ever.

WOMEN

He is getting stronger.

> *CREAM is out of the tomb, decayed but still dapper in a tuxedo, white gloves with cane.*

THE DEAD

As long as you believe.

WOMEN

He is alive in you.

THE DEAD

As long as you believe.

WOMEN
Deep in your memory.

CREAM
I welcome you here.

WOMEN
Deep in your memory.

CREAM
I worship your fear.

WOMEN
Deep in your memory he dwells.

CREAM
I do not know if I wish you well.

WOMEN
Deep in your memory.

CREAM
I welcome you here.

WOMEN
Deep in your memory.

CREAM
I worship your fear.

WOMEN
Deep in your memory he dwells.

CREAM
A bloody kiss from a wishing well-well-well-hello-hello-hello-hello all those familiar faces. Yes and time-time-time is a very strange thing my friends and even the words that I said just now are nothing more than a memory. But whoever, whenever, wherever, I bid you all good evening at this moment at this time, at this place right here and now at

McGill—"McGill, James, James McGill, he's our faw-ther, oh yes rawther, James, James McGill..." He got all this land through fraud, don't you know? Thirty-eight thousand acres of it. The original crime, the modus operandi, the Honourable James, James McGill. But we don't talk about such things, do we gentlemen? Those things that are done in secret. The lies that are buried in the basement, lies oozing through the cracks in the walls, dripping down from the ceiling, leaking from the windows, poisoning the ivy, staining the lawn.

WOMEN

Lies.

CREAM

Lies.

WOMEN

Lies.

CREAM

And verily I say unto you that the Wages of Sin is Death...like your little servant girl and his mistress, little French girl, wasn't it? And you cried when she died, didn't you? You cried boo-hoo-hoo-thank you very much doctor, thank you very much. But no, we don't talk about such things, do we, gentlemen? We don't talk about why you had me erased, oh yes, from your bibliographies, purged from your official histories and expelled from my profession. A man who was your friend and associate, who shared your dreams and ambitions and helped you create the McGill that we have today. A McGill that lies, a McGill that cheats, a McGill that has very good reasons for hiding the fact that I ever existed, because I am the only one who knows the truth, the whole truth and nothing but the truth about these fair and gentle creatures that you see before you—all dead-dead-dead- before their time and leaving not even a whisper of an echo of a shadow of themselves in the history of this school, even though the murder of these young women did shape the very form and substance of this

19

institution. A story that has been suppressed because its details do tend to incriminate some who have been honoured by McGill as humanitarian benefactors. But I want you to know what they really are and I want you to know who I am.

WOMEN
(Singing)

I'm not a Doc
I'm not a Yid
Nor yet a foreign skipper
But I am your true loving friend
Yours truly, Jack the Ripper.

CREAM
I was born little Thomas Neill Cream, don't you know, ladies? The son of a successful businessman, dealing in lumber by the foot and by the yard. Dear old daddy. "Spare the Rod and Spoil the Child." As the eldest son I was expected to carry on the family business but it soon became apparent that I had other inclinations. A fascination, let's say, with the inner functionings of the mind and body, which led me to register, against my father's protests, as a student of Medicine at McGill. There I began my training in the University Lying-In Hospital, a Charity Hospital for the Poor and Destitute, located on Rue Saint Dominique, right in the heart of Montreal's red-light district.

WOMEN
Satan's Circus.

CREAM
Satan's Circus.

WOMEN
Looking for a good time, doctor?

CREAM
It was there that Sir Willie Osler began building his reputation as a world expert in Social Diseases. A bright

20

young man, only a few years older than myself, but how
different we were.

> OSLER

Yes, I remember Cream. A good student from a very
respectable family who did work well with me, despite the
rumours about his activities as a man about town. The fact
that Cream might be indulging himself somewhat with
members of the opposite sex did not particularly upset me.
Nor did I speak out when I heard that Cream might be
performing abortions, a practice not too uncommon
amongst medical students trying to pay their way through
college. But then there was the question of Nati Mascou.

WOMAN ONE sits on the floor.

> OSLER

A young native girl, stabbed in the lower abdomen, slashed
about her thighs, her dress, her stockings soaked with
blood.

> CREAM

Blood.

> NATI

Wotshima.

> OSLER

She said.

> NATI

Wotshima.

> OSLER

It meant nothing to me.

> CREAM

It means nothing to you?

OSLER

I only remember the tone of her voice and the way she said the word.

NATI

Wotshima.

OSLER

Who are you?

THE DEAD

(Echo) Who are you?

OSLER

Your name.

THE DEAD

Your name.

OSLER

Your name.

CREAM

Then I saw the necklace and I knew who she was.

OSLER

We must call the police.

CREAM

He said and I shrugged.

OSLER

Then he smiled.

CREAM

I smiled.

NATI

Wotshima.

OSLER

What does it mean?

CREAM

(To OSLER) Do you really want to know?

NATI

Wotshima.

CREAM

(To audience) Do you really want to know?

WOMEN

(Doing a native chant) Ay-yah-ay-et-et-et-et Ay-yah-yah-yah-yah-et-et-etay-ya-ay-et-et-etay-yah-yah-yah-yah-et-et-etay-yah-yah-yah-et-et-et-ET-ET.

STRATHCONA leaves his pedestal and approaches the centre.

CREAM

Lord Strathcona to the tower came.

WOMEN 2, 3

Lord Strathcona.

CREAM

Born into a world in the pangs of sorting itself out, into the monstrously rich and the abysmally poor.

WOMEN 2, 3

Strathcona he goes.

CREAM

Strengthening himself with passages learnt by heart from his book—a dark, fate-ridden young hero.

WOMEN 2, 3

To conquer the world.

STRATHCONA
And Scotland was hellfire and damnation.

CREAM
Scotland was oatmeal and fog.

STRATHCONA
Scotland was a place to leave.

WOMEN 2, 3
Scotland.

CREAM
A lumber ship on the Atlantic, a packet carrying immigrants. All of them like you or me, but none of them like Lord Strathcona.

WOMEN 2, 3
He knows what he wants.

CREAM
In his heart and in his mind.

WOMEN 2, 3
He knows what he wants.

CREAM
And his eyes reflect only what he wants the people to see. And he sees only what he needs.

WOMEN 2, 3
Only what he needs.

STRATHCONA takes a position with the lanterns and does a prayer with the rest of THE DEAD.

STRATHCONA
O God of Bethel.

THE DEAD

By Whose hand.

STRATHCONA

Thy people still are fed.

THE DEAD

Who through this weary pilgrimage.

STRATHCONA

Hast all our fathers led.

THE DEAD

O God of Bethel.

STRATHCONA

By Whose hand He created a world possessed by Satan and
the whole world is Satan.

THE DEAD

And Satan is the world.

STRATHCONA

And the world cannot go on without usury.

THE DEAD

Without avarice.

STRATHCONA

Without pride.

THE DEAD

Without whoring.

STRATHCONA

Without murder.

THE DEAD

Without all manner of sin.

STRATHCONA

Otherwise the world would cease to be the world.

THE DEAD

And the Devil without the Devil.

STRATHCONA

And money is the word of the Devil through which he creates all things.

THE DEAD

No black without white.

STRATHCONA

No day without night.

THE DEAD

"There is a dreadful hell of corrosive pain
Where sinners must, with devils dwell
In darkness, fire and chains."

CREAM

And Strathcona came to Montreal in 1838 with a letter of introduction to Sir George Simpson, the head factor and London Governor of the Hudson's Bay Company, "claiming the sole trade of all those seas, straits, bays, rivers, lakes, creeks and sounds that are not already actually possessed by or granted to any of their associates."

SIMPSON approaches STRATHCONA in the centre.

WOMEN 2, 3

Sir George Simpson.

SIMPSON

Well, Strathcona.

STRATHCONA

He said.

SIMPSON

Other people might believe that the Hudson's Bay
Company has been ordained so that more churches might
be built so that Indians might live better, more Christian
lives. But our job, sir, is to make one hundred percent
profit on our shareholders' money. As for the natives, sir,
they are nothing more than a filthy rabble, sir, a bloody
bunch of savages and they smell, sir, they smell.

STRATHCONA

Then he dismissed me.

SIMPSON

Please show Strathcona the fur room and instruct him in
the art of counting—

STRATHCONA

Ratskins.

WOMAN 2

Raccoon.

WOMAN 3

Lynx.

WOMAN 2

Otter.

WOMAN 3

Fox.

WOMAN 2

Marlet.

WOMAN 3

Mink.

WOMAN 2

Sable.

CREAM

And that sweet furry thing that made all of this possible...

WOMEN 2, 3

The Beaver.

CREAM

"Pro Pelle Cutem."

WOMAN 2, 3

Skin for skin.

CREAM

Mitts, muffs, collars, coats, wraps, and cute little sealskin caps, like the one Lady Simpson made fashionable, tilted just slightly over her coiffure so sweet and sassy and la-de-dah.

WOMEN 2, 3

La-de-dah.

WOMAN Two does Lady Simpson.

THE DEAD

"Rule Britannia."

CREAM

Ah yes, there's no tart like an old tart.

THE DEAD

"Britannia rules the waves."

WOMAN 2

"And what if the best of our wages be
An empty sleeve, a stiff set knee
A crutch for the rest of life, who cares
As long as the one flag floats and dares
As long as the One Race dares and grows
Death, what is Death but God's own rose
Let but the bugles of England play
Over the hills and far, far away."

28

THE DEAD
"Rule Britannia over Pine and Palm."

STRATHCONA
And I worked, I saved and studied. Studied, worked and saved my time and money.

WOMEN 2, 3
Money and time.

STRATHCONA
Reading Plutarch's *Lives* and *The Correspondence of Benjamin Franklin* in the frozen wilderness of Labrador.

WOMEN 2, 3
Year after year after year.

CREAM
A stitch in time.

WOMEN 2, 3
Saves nine.

CREAM
A penny saved.

WOMEN 2, 3
Is a penny earned.

CREAM
A bird in the hand.

WOMEN 2, 3
Is worth two in the bush.

CREAM
And it's never too late to learn.

STRATHCONA
I didn't make the rules. I obeyed them.

CREAM

And other men died of scurvy, drink and starvation. They drowned, they froze, they went blind. A bite from a mosquito could scratch into a fester. The festering could spread into a fever and the fever into a sweat. Then the man would die, killed by mosquito.

WOMEN 2, 3

But Strathcona lived.

STRATHCONA

I obeyed.

WOMEN 2, 3

O God of Bethel, by Whose hand.

STRATHCONA

I obeyed.

CREAM

Transforming pain, courage, faith, blood, shit and mud into streams of gold.

WOMEN 2, 3

Year after year after year.

STRATHCONA

I learnt to think in terms of business and forced myself to think only on the business side of what I was doing, or else go mad.

Dong.

THE DEAD

Seven o'clock bell.

NATI

Manitoupeewanisque, we called him, the Man of Iron Spirit. And at first we welcomed him with his gun, his blankets, his medicine and our chief said we must obey his rules. We must listen to our white brothers and believe in his God. And that's when we began to die.

STRATHCONA

I heard reports of the Indians trading goods on their own, bartering with other tribes. This was not permitted by the company and I told them I would have to stop all supplies. I warned them.

NATI

And our hunters had to travel further and further into the north to find the beaver and many did not come back.

STRATHCONA

They died hungry in the snow.

NATI

And we died hungry outside the fort.

Dong.

THE DEAD

Eight o'clock bell.

STRATHCONA

I had to lock the fort gate that year, after they tried to kill their chief. A murderous world, a filthy rabble, who left their sick to die and ate their own children, bled them for their blood. And in the horror of all that suffering, O Lord, I did question you. I questioned you, O Lord.

NATI

And the women outside chanting.

WOMEN 2, 3

Wotshima.

NATI

Open the door.

WOMEN 2, 3

Wotshima.

NATI

Open your heart.

WOMEN 2, 3

Wotshima.

NATI

Hear us, Wotshima.

WOMEN 2, 3

Hear us in our suffering.

NATI

And let us live.

WOMEN 2, 3

Do not let us die.

NATI

Do not let us die.

WOMEN 2, 3

O sisters.

NATI

And it could have been you.

WOMEN 2, 3

It could have been me.

NATI

It could have been you.

WOMEN 2, 3

It could have been me.

WOMEN

(Together) O sisters.

NATI

In sorrow I am speaking, O Four Powers of the Earth. Of the North, of the South, of the East, of the West, hear me in my sorrow for I may never speak again.

WOMEN

(Together) O let my people live.

Dong.

THE DEAD

Nine o'clock bell.

NATI

You don't know me, you never heard of me. There are no cities, no buildings, no mountains named after me. But I am a face that you have seen before. The wooden Indian, the drunken Indian, came out of me. I was a victim. I did what I was told.

STRATHCONA

Nati Mascou.

NATI

I went to Montreal with Wotshima, where I worked as a servant girl. I washed. I cooked. I cleaned and at night I would sit in my room.

STRATHCONA

She would sit in her room.

NATI

I was lonely.

STRATHCONA

She was sad.

NATI

And sometimes at night I would sing my songs, the songs of my people.

STRATHCONA

Like a ghost at the window.

NATI

I would look up at the stars and sing.

STRATHCONA

She was beautiful.

NATI

And sometimes Wotshima, he would look at me. A cold look, a hard look, like he was angry and I was afraid.

WOMEN 2, 3

O sisters.

NATI

I was afraid.

STRATHCONA

O God of Bethel by Whose hand.

Dong.

THE DEAD

Ten o'clock bell.

NATI

And he would stand in the hall way every night. He would stand outside my door. One hour, two hours.

WOMEN 2, 3

Are you coming to bed, dear?

NATI

He put his hand on the door and he bowed his head.

WOMEN 2, 3

Manitoupeewanisque.

NATI

Man of Iron Spirit.

WOMEN 2, 3

Wotshima.

NATI

"The First One."

WOMEN 2, 3

He bowed his head and cried.

THE DEAD

O God of Bethel.

STRATHCONA

By Whose hand.

NATI

And he was cold, so cold.

WOMEN 2, 3

What is it that you want, Wotshima?

NATI

And he pulled back the covers on the bed.

WOMEN 2, 3

What is it that you want?

STRATHCONA

And I would stand in the hallway every night. I would stand outside her door. One hour, two hours.

WOMEN 2, 3

Are you coming to bed dear?

STRATHCONA

And I put my hand on the door and I bowed my head.

WOMEN 2, 3

Manitoupeewanisque.

NATI

Man of Iron Spirit.

WOMEN 2, 3

Wotshima.

NATI

"The First One."

STRATHCONA

I bowed my head and cried.

THE DEAD

O God of Bethel.

WOMEN 2, 3

By Whose hand.

STRATHCONA

And I was cold, so cold.

NATI

What is it that you want, Wotshima?

STRATHCONA

And I pulled back the covers on the bed.

NATI

What is it that you want?

STRATHCONA raises his hand.

GUIDE

Exhibit Number One.

GUIDE holds up a knife.

WOMEN 2, 3
Exhibit Number One

GUIDE
A knife of the sort issued and sold by the Hudson's Bay Company. Horn handle with an iron blade, used for scraping and slicing.

WOMEN 2, 3
Ripping and gutting.

GUIDE
Fish and fowl.

WOMEN 2, 3
Friend and foe.

GUIDE
Your knife, Strathcona.

WOMEN 2, 3
Your knife.

GUIDE places the knife in STRATHCONA's upraised hand.

STRATHCONA
It was my hand upon the knife. It was my knife that did the deed. But what drove the knife. What drove the hand?

THE DEAD
If she lives, we die.

STRATHCONA
If she dies, we live.

STRATHCONA raises the knife to striking point.

WOMEN 2, 3

(Building to a crescendo) And in the city there is a street and in the street there is a house and in the house there is a room and in the room there is a bed and in the bed there is a woman and in the woman there is a—

STRATHCONA *lowers the knife.*

THE DEAD

Knife.

WOMEN 2, 3
(Doing motions)

"X marks the spot
with a circle and a dot
The knife goes in, the knife comes out
The blood rushes up, the blood rushes down
The blood rushes all around—You're dead!"

WOMEN TWO *and* THREE *point at the audience.*

Dong.

THE DEAD

Eleven o'clock bell.

WOMEN

(Together) Remember.

CREAM

"When inoffensive people plant a dagger in your breast your good is what they really want, they do it for the best."

GUIDE

Exhibit Number Two.

WOMEN 1, 3

Exhibit Number Two.

GUIDE

A bone necklace belonging to Nati Mascou. *(GUIDE hands necklace to CREAM.)*

OSLER

I watched Cream take the necklace and I followed him out of the hospital.

CREAM

In November, in the rain.

OSLER

A natty dresser.

WOMEN 2, 3

Neill Cream.

OSLER

A dapper Dan, stepping lightly up the street out of the smoke and dirt of the lower town into Westmount, along Dorchester Street.

CREAM

In the night.

OSLER

In the wind.

CREAM

In the last yellow leaves blowing wet along the sidewalks.

WOMEN 2, 3

Hello, Doctor Cream.

OSLER

And I wasn't sure what I was doing. I told myself, go back to the hospital, go back to your studies, go back to your career and the life you have planned because this can only hurt you. But I stood on the corner and I waited. I waited and saw the lights go on in the windows of the second floor. I saw the shadows of who and what and why would the blood of a young girl lead to this house?

WOMEN
(Together) The house of Lord Strathcona.

STRATHCONA sitting down on his pedestal.

CREAM
Strathcona was sitting in his study, looking very much like the portrait of himself that hangs in the Royal Victoria College. The same frosty blue eyes and that cold, cold exterior of a man of absolute control. I could see he was mad. He was totally insane.

STRATHCONA
Well, Mr. Cream.

CREAM
He said.

STRATHCONA
You don't know me, but I know you.

CREAM
And who am I, sir?

STRATHCONA
You sir, are a blackmailer, an abortionist and a very ambitious young man.

CREAM
Indeed, sir.

STRATHCONA
Indeed.

CREAM holds up the necklace.

CREAM

And this?

STRATHCONA

Is she alive?

CREAM

Oh yes.

STRATHCONA

A fine necklace, Mr. Cream. The Nascapi make them out of caribou teeth. They live off the caribou, they worship the caribou, the Nascapi. And when the caribou die, they die. Do you understand, Mr. Cream? No, you don't. You don't understand. The Hamilton Inlet, Rigolet, Besiamets, all of these are just names to you, but I was the man. I was there in the cold, in the wind, in the darkness of the night, in Labrador, sir, where the native people do it like animals on the ground. Here or there, where they please, when they please, with whom they please. But O Lord, I kept Thy Commandment, I resisted all temptations, until tonight...and the stupid bitch wouldn't die. Blood all over the bed, blood all over the floor, blood all up and down the stairs, blood!...now what can I do for you, Mr. Cream? What can I do for you?

CREAM

I await your pleasure, sir.

STRATHCONA

Then I have one more question, Mr. Cream. Will she live? Will she live, Mr. Cream?

CREAM

And I could have said yes, but I said what he wanted to hear.

WOMEN 2, 3

No.

CREAM

No.

WOMEN 2, 3

No.

CREAM hands STRATHCONA the necklace.

CREAM

And I knew that this was it. The one and only opportunity that could possibly push and place me above my intended fate and destiny in life, at this rather critical point in my career when certain gentlemen at McGill were threatening to expose my situation. But, oh no, that was not to be.

STRATHCONA

When you return, Mr. Cream, we will discuss our business arrangements in further detail?

CREAM

Sir.

STRATHCONA

Providing, of course, that our little transaction proves successful and there are no accidents. I do not believe in accidents, Mr. Cream.

CREAM

I think we understand each other, sir.

STRATHCONA

Yes, I think we do.

CREAM

Yes.

STRATHCONA

Yes.

WOMEN
Yes.

CREAM turns away from STRATHCONA.

OSLER
I watched Cream step out of the house as the moon came
up behind the Notre Dame Cathedral.

CREAM
A pale white light behind the clouds.

WOMEN 2, 3
Taking a stroll, Doctor Cream?

CREAM locks arms with the two WOMEN.

OSLER
I think he even glanced my way and smiled.

GUIDE
"The McGill Cakewalk Song."

CREAM
(Singing)
I'm a sweet man
A discreet man
I can cut a deal with you
woo-wooo
And leave no clues
who-who-who
I'll do it nice, a sacrifice
Mmmmmm-mmmmm
I'm a lover
Undercover
I can hoochie-coochie-smoochie-woochie-woo
Woo-woo
I make it last
ooo-oo-oo
To their last gasp

Mmmm-mmm-mmm
When I walk
I walk alone
When I talk
You shiver in your bones
A drop in stock
Can lead to shock
What can we do?
boo-hoo
Too bad for you boo-hoo

WOMEN
(Singing)

He's a sweet man
A discreet man
He can cut a deal with you
woo-woo
and leave no clues
ooo-ooo
He'll do it nice
A sacrifice
Mmmmmm-mmmmm
He's a lover
undercover
He can woochie-coochie-smoochie-woochie-woo
woo-woo
He'll make it last
Oooo-ooo-oo
To your last gasp
Mmm-mmm-mmmm

CREAM

When I walk
I walk alone

WOMEN

When he talks
You shiver in your bones

44

CREAM

A drop in stock
can lead to shocks
ahhhhhhhhhhhhhhh
what can we do?
boo-hoo
Too bad for you

WOMEN

Boo-hoo
what can they do?
boo-hoo
Too bad for you

OSLER

I followed him down into the lower town, where he stopped
in Place d'Armes and looked up at the Bank of Montreal.
Just stood there, looking at it.

CREAM

Oh yes, I was ambitious. A young man, a young British
gentleman at the very time and peak of the British Empire.
And I wanted the Good Life. I wanted my share of the
power and the glory, and the fuck and the suck and the
moan and the groan of it. And did you think we were only
photographs? Did you think we were very much different
from you?

OSLER

Cream!

CREAM

Why Doctor Osler, what brings you here?

WOMEN 2, 3

Wee-Willie-Wee-Wee-Willie-Wee-Willie.

OSLER

Laughing, he was laughing

CREAM

Chercher les femmes, doctor?

OSLER

Cream, I demand to know what is going on here?

CREAM

Oh, he demands to know.

WOMEN laugh.

Why I thought you had already guessed by now, Doctor Osler?

OSLER

You realize, sir, that I must not only inform your family but the authorities about your unorthodox behavior. *(They laugh.)* Do you think I am joking, sir?

CREAM

Oh, I know he was not joking.

OSLER

I am waiting, Cream.

CREAM

And I said I was willing to reveal all, to make a complete and shameful confession about my situation. But, I was worried, I am concerned, Doctor Osler, about the other names I would have to mention.

OSLER

What are the names?

CREAM

Are you sure, Doctor Osler?

OSLER

What are the names, sir?

CREAM

I smiled and gave him the names of some students from some very prominent families indeed, didn't I, Sir Wee Willie?

OSLER

You are lying, Cream. Are you lying to me?

CREAM

And I offered to show him some photographs.

OSLER

No, I said no.

CREAM

And clearly it was his duty, by his own standards and code of honour to report this information to the authorities, despite the damage it would cause to the school, to the city, to his position.

OSLER

Or else be forever condemned by my own conscience.

CREAM

But he let me go.

OSLER

I let him go.

WOMEN and CREAM laugh.

OSLER

This is a nightmare.

WOMEN 2, 3

You are going to wake up.

OSLER

This is a nightmare.

WOMEN 2, 3

You are going to wake up.

CREAM

Wake up.

WOMEN 2, 3

"If you ever see a hearse go by
Remember that you are the next to die
They'll put you in a big black box
And cover you with mud and rocks
The worms crawl in, the worms crawl out
They'll creep in your nose—

THE DEAD

—and crawl out your mouth!"

GUIDE

Exhibit Number Three. *(GUIDE holds up a glass bottle.)* A glass bottle containing six ounces of chloroform. A colourless heavy fluid with an ether-like scent, used as a solvent and anaesthetic.

WOMEN

(Together) By Doctor Thomas Neill Cream.

GUIDE hands the bottle to CREAM.

STRATHCONA

Now is the time.

CREAM

To remember.

STRATHCONA

Now is the time.

CREAM

In November.

STRATHCONA

Now is the time.

CREAM

Now.

CREAM takes his position.

OSLER

Oh yes, I was there. I saw it. I knew what was happening, but what could I do? There was nothing I could do. I mean, who was going to admit in Victorian Montreal that this, all of this, was actually possible? And even if I could prove it, who would listen to me? Who could I talk to, who could I appeal to on a subject that nobody wanted to know about?

CREAM

Nobody.

OSLER

And I had to shut it out. I had to put it out of my mind, otherwise you never would have heard of me. There would have been no Sir William Osler.

WOMEN 2, 3

There would have been no Osler Library.

OSLER

It was simply a question of being somewhere I shouldn't have been. Seeing something I shouldn't have seen. Something that I would soon forget in the course of my career. And I believe I made the right decision, the only decision that I could have made, because, despite all our faults and failings, we of McGill did make progress in education and sciences. We moved the world forward.

CREAM

But how could he know, how could he guess where that progress would lead us. But I knew.

Lights up on the memorial windows.

WOMEN 2, 3

Ypres.

THE DEAD

The Somme.

WOMEN 2, 3

Arras.

THE DEAD

Cambrai.

WOMEN 2, 3

Vimy Ridge.

THE DEAD

Vimy Ridge.

WOMEN

Passchendaele.

THE DEAD

Passchendaele.

CREAM takes the stopper off the bottle.

CREAM
(Singing softly)

Beautiful dreamer
Wake unto me
Starlight and dewdrops
Are waiting for thee
Sounds of the rude world
Heard in the day
Lulled by the moonlight
Have all passed away.

OSLER

And she died softly

CREAM

Good night.

OSLER

She died softly.

CREAM

Good night.

OSLER

Good night.

WOMEN

O sisters.

NATI

Mother-mother.

WOMEN 2, 3

May I go across the river?

NATI

To get the golden slipper?

WOMEN 2, 3

Mother-mother.

NATI

May I go across the river?

WOMEN 2, 3

To get the golden slipper?

NATI

Not unless you have—

                         WOMEN 2, 3
Not unless you have—

                         NATI
Not unless you have—

                         THE DEAD
The colour black.

         NATI bows her head in death.

                         GUIDE
Exhibit Number Four

                         WOMAN 2, 3
Exhibit Number Four.

         GUIDE holds up a glass jar.

                         GUIDE
Glass jar marked "kidney, liver and stomach of Nati
Mascou."

                         OSLER
Kidney.

                         CREAM
Four ounces.

                         OSLER
Liver.

                         CREAM
Five-and-a-half ounces.

                         OSLER
Stomach.

                         CREAM
Ten-and-a-half ounces.

OSLER

Stomach and contents.

CREAM

Very acid, had gastric odor with other viscera normal.
There was some hypostasis, though not actually putrid.

OSLER

Died, November 1872.

Takes off the rubber gloves.

CREAM

Murder an unnatural act? Good friends, it is by criminal
things and deeds unnatural that nature works and has its
being. And what evil is here for us to do when the whole
body of things is evil? The spider kills the fly and calls it a
crime? And what are the worst sins we can do, we who live
for a day and die in a night? A few murders...?

STRATHCONA approaches CREAM.

STRATHCONA

And nobody knows.

CREAM

Nobody can prove anything.

STRATHCONA

Nobody knows.

CREAM

Nobody can prove anything.

STRATHCONA

Nobody knows.

WOMAN 2

But the proof is here, right here at McGill, if you know
where to look for it. Or rather, how to look at it. For

example, did Lord Strathcona actually kill someone called Nati Mascou? Or is she just a fictional character, a figment of our imagination? We know that in a court of law, Lord Strathcona would be declared innocent, but do you believe that? Or is it just something you want to believe? Because if this is true, then who are you?

WOMEN

Take a closer look. *(The* WOMEN *exit, chanting the song "Untimely Life" around the audience.)*

> Untimely life, untimely death
> How close are you to your last breath
> Darkness in life, darkness in death
> How close are you to your last breath.

Lights go up as the GUIDE *takes central position near the tomb of James McGill.*

GUIDE

Comrades and friends, we will now recess for fifteen minutes in order to consider the evidence brought against the Illustrious Dead of McGill in the murder of Nati Mascou.

During the fifteen minute intermission the audience can tour the museum and review the information it presents. A change of light and sound of wind as the GUIDE *once again takes the central position at the tomb of James McGill.*

GUIDE

Comrades and friends, having presented the evidence against the Illustrious Dead of McGill in the murder of Nati Mascou, we will now continue with our story. Beginning on a night in November 1873, or rather, let us consider the memories of someone looking back at that year from right here and now. Nothing ever really dies, it only changes.

Light change as WOMAN TWO *steps forward, transformed by a simple change of costume into a more masculine-looking*

54

figure. She is singing "The Internationale" in a quiet manner as she strolls along.

ARMAND
"Debout les damnés de la terre"

VOICES
(Echoing) —Damnés de la terre

ARMAND
"Debout les forçats de la faim"

VOICES
(Echoing) —Forçats de la faim

ARMAND
"La raison tonne en son cratère"

VOICES
(Echoing) —Cratère

ARMAND
"C'est l'éruption de la fin"

VOICES
(Echoing) —Fin-fin-fin-fin-fin

The lines of all the French characters can be delivered in French.

ARMAND
"The Internationale," you don't hear it much any more. "Arise ye prisoners of Starvation." Well, socialism is dead, they say. It is the end of history, there will be no more changes. Capitalism has triumphed, now and forever. That's what they used to tell us too, heh, back when I was living around here. Was I a man or a woman? Black or white, French or English? Ce ne fait rien, I was a worker. Doing twelve hours a day, six days a week for a dollar a day. Digging the ditches, collecting the garbage, delivering the

goods, cutting the cloth, we did it all, oui. We built this city. We built this school, not them, heh? But there are no portraits of me, no photographs, no plaques on the wall honouring any of us for being alive. But the facts are there if you want to read them. The statistics on the birth rates, the death rates, the unemployment rates and even some of the houses and factories we worked and lived in are still standing in Pointe Saint Charles where I grew up.

CAMILLE

Joseph Armand.

ARMAND

Living with family down there on Murray Street near the scrap yards in a tenement house with a broken door and a face that looks out a window. Ma soeur, Camille.

CREAM
(Appearing)
"Of all the girls that are so smart
There's none like pretty Sally
She is the darling of my heart
And she lives down in our alley
Sally, Sally, in our alley
She's the sunshine of Paradise Lane."

ARMAND

Much too pretty for Pointe Saint Charles.

CAMILLE

And sometimes I'd walk uptown along clean streets where people bowed and tipped their hats at the ladies. *(CREAM tips his hat.)* They didn't push, they didn't shove, they smiled at you.

CAMILLE strolling.

CREAM

Those eyes, that hair, those hips, that mouth.

WOMAN 1

Too bad.

ARMAND

So sad.

CREAM

She's only a working girl.

CAMILLE

But I was different, I knew I was different.

ARMAND

She had dreams, she had ambitions.

CAMILLE

I wanted to be a lady. I wanted to live.

ARMAND

You are making a mistake, Camille.

CAMILLE

I want to live.

CREAM

Her real name was Brigitte. It was I who named her Camille after Our Lady of the Flowers. A little factory girl when I met her. Quite ready to give it away, but oh no, my dear. You must not be shy of accepting gifts from strangers if you wish to get ahead in the world.

CREAM holds out a flower.

ARMAND

No, Camille.

CREAM

For your hair, mademoiselle.

CAMILLE takes the flower.

ARMAND

Me, I was working as a docker. All day I worked unloading the Molson Ale, Redpath Sugar, Oglivie Flour, MacDonald Tobacco, from ships belonging to Sir Hugh Allan. *(Lights up on ALLAN.)* He never went home dirty, I did. My clothes, my shirt, I could never get it off my hands.

CAMILLE

Joseph.

ARMAND

In the cold weather, when the ice blocked up the river, they'd lay us off. Just like that, heh? Good-bye, that's all. They don't give a shit, heh? We are not human to them. We're still not human to them. We only live to work.

CAMILLE

Joseph, I am going out tonight.

ARMAND

There was no father at home. Our mother, all she did was work and pray, work and pray, but Jesus he did nothing for us, heh? It's me that fed the kids.

CAMILLE

Do you like my new dress?

ARMAND

I couldn't blame her.

CREAM

Call me a pimp? An exploiter of women? Why the poor dears begged me to use them, didn't you? After all, what I had to offer was better than working in a factory, better than being a wife. The dirty dishes, the dirty diapers, the drunken husband and a frown on the face that gets deeper and deeper.

CAMILLE

I don't want to be like you, Mama.

WOMAN 1 & CAMILLE
I don't want to be like you.

ARMAND
And none of us knew it but we were all put on a schedule
that was set when Sir George Etienne Cartier moved in the
House of Commons that it go into committee on a
resolution that a Pacific Railway be constructed by private
enterprise from coast to coast.

ALLAN
From the Atlantic to the Pacific.

CREAM
A railway that would be absolutely vital in terms of trade
and revenue to Montreal and the whole of Canada.

STRATHCONA
And it seems reasonable to assume, Mr. Cream, that Sir
Hugh, who has been assiduously cultivating his connections
with Sir John A. MacDonald and the Conservative Party
over the last twenty years, will receive the said government
contract, unless, Mr. Cream, you and the other agents that I
have employed can supply me with proof that Sir Hugh or
any of his associates have or are now involved in activities
that might be considered morally apprehensive by the
Electorate of this nation.

CREAM
Whispers and secrets that I overheard.

WOMEN
In Room Two Hundred and Two.

CREAM
The walls talk back at you.

WOMEN
In Room Two Hundred and Two.

CREAM
The walls talk back at you.

WOMEN
In Room Two Hundred and Two.

CREAM
(*Holds out card to member of the audience*) Allow mc to present you with my card, sir. Doctor Thomas Neill Cream, Master of Ceremonies at the Elite Club, located for your convenience and pleasure, sir, at One Sixty-Seven La Gauchetiere Street West. Just around the corner from the Bank of Montreal, with services recommended by many distinguished gentlemen in our fair city.

WOMEN
Satisfaction guaranteed.

CREAM
In the privacy of your own room.

WOMEN
Chacun à son goût.

CREAM
Allow yourself to pick and choose.

WOMAN 1
Fuck.

WOMAN 2
Suck.

WOMAN 3
Hump.

WOMEN
(*Together*) Screw.

CREAM
No matter what, no matter who.

WOMEN
It's what we like, it's what we do.

CREAM
The saucy Josie.

WOMAN ONE poses herself seductively.

CREAM
She likes it hot, she likes it hard. She's everything your heart desires.

WOMAN 3
More.

WOMAN 2
More.

WOMAN 1
More.

WOMEN
(Together) That's what we're here for.

CREAM
And sweet Louise.

WOMAN TWO poses herself seductively.

CREAM
For those who like them young and tender.

WOMAN 1
Oh no.

WOMAN 3
Oh no.

WOMAN 2

Oh no.

CREAM

She moans in soft surrender.

WOMEN

(Together) I want you.

CREAM

And the sublime Camille.

WOMAN THREE poses herself seductively as CAMILLE.

CREAM

For those who have a bit of taste
Then this young lady's worth the wait
She's the one that likes to treat
A connoisseur beneath the sheets.

WOMAN 3

Suf-fer.

WOMEN 1, 2

Eat your heart out, sucker.

CREAM

What is your pleasure?

WOMEN

Where is the pain?

CREAM

What is your pleasure?

WOMEN

Where is the pain?

CREAM

Chacun à son goût is the motto of our game.

LAURIER
(Masked, points at CAMILLE) That one.

WOMEN 1, 2
"Shame, shame, double shame
Now we know your girlfriend's name."

CREAM
Masks, gentlemen, please.

WOMEN 1, 2
Masks, gentlemen, please.

THE DEAD put on surgical masks.

CREAM
Gloves.

WOMEN 1, 2
Gloves.

THE DEAD put on surgical gloves.

CREAM
We will now proceed with the operation according to the
instructions of Doctor Richard von Kraftt-Ebing.

*WOMEN ONE and TWO as nurses on either side of the
operating table, where LAURIER has mounted CAMILLE. THE
DEAD are standing behind the table in a semi-circle as
observers.*

CREAM
"The act of Cohabitation." *(Quoting from the book,
"Psychopathia Sexualis")* "Gentlemen, the propagation of the
human race is not left to mere accident or the caprices of
the individual, but is guaranteed by the hidden laws of
nature which are enforced by a mighty and irresistible
impulse."

THE DEAD groan.

CREAM

"However, the real object of the sexual instinct, i.e. the propagation of the species, is not always present to the mind during the act and the impulse is stronger than it could be justified by the gratification that can possibly be derived from it."

THE DEAD groan and LAURIER begins to heave rhythmically.

CREAM

"The essential condition for the male is sufficient erection of the penis."

WOMAN 1

The cock.

WOMAN 2

The prick.

WOMAN 1

The tool.

CREAM

"And during the sexual act, the erection of the penis leads to a nervous excitement which is distributed over the entire vasomotor system of nerves."

THE DEAD and LAURIER begin heaving in earnest as Cream, no longer looking at the book, steps towards the audience in measured paces.

CREAM

"This excitement results in a turgescence of the organs—inflection of the conjuctiva—prominence of the eyeballs—dilation of the pupils—cardiac palpitations—increased stimulation which results—in—pleasurable feelings—evoked—by—the—passing—of—semen—through—the ductus—ejaculatory—to—the—

THE DEAD, LAURIER and CREAM climax.

THE DEAD, LAURIER, CREAM

(Together) —U—RETHRA."

CAMILLE screams.

LAURIER turns around and faces the audience after taking off his mask.

WOMEN 1, 2

Daddy.

THE DEAD

Don't hit me.

WOMEN 1, 2

Daddy.

THE DEAD

Don't hit me.

CREAM

Case Number One.

WOMEN 1, 2

Case Number One.

One of THE DEAD, still wearing the surgical mask and gloves, approaches centre stage.

CREAM

Sir George Etienne Cartier, under pressure concerning certain financial obligations, would, from time to time, go to a house of prostitution, enter a room with a girl, then wistfully regard her shoes.

THE DEAD

Taken by lust.

CREAM

He kisses and bites one of the shoes, then presses the shoe
against his genitals. Ejaculates the semen and rubs his
armpit and chest with the semen.

WOMEN 1, 2

Mommy.

THE DEAD

Don't leave me.

WOMEN 1, 2

Mommy.

THE DEAD

Don't leave me.

> SIR GEORGE *exits as another one of* THE DEAD *approaches the
> centre.*

CREAM

Case Number Two.

WOMEN 1, 2

Case Number Two.

CREAM

Sir John A. Macdonald, shocked after hearing from Sir
George about certain facts and figures, became very
restless, irritable and was apprehended one day in a shop in
the act of frottage on a lady.

THE DEAD

Taken by lust.

CREAM

He was very repentant and asked to be severely punished
for his irresistible impulse.

WOMEN 1, 2

Mommy.

THE DEAD

I'm afraid of the dark.

WOMEN 1, 2

Mommy.

THE DEAD

I'm afraid of the dark.

Sir John A. exits as Sir Hugh approaches centre stage, still wearing his surgical mask.

CREAM

Case Number Three.

WOMEN 1, 2

Case Number Three.

CREAM

He wasn't one of our regulars, but every once in a while, in a private room with a private exit, he would choose his girl. The Pin-Man, we called him.

WOMEN

The Pin-Man.

CREAM

One at a time.

WOMAN 1

In the arms.

WOMAN 2

In the legs.

WOMAN 3

In the breasts.

                    WOMEN
Pain.

                    CREAM
Pain.

                    WOMEN
Pain.

                    ALLAN
Does it hurt?

                    WOMEN
Yes.

                    ALLAN
Does it hurt?

                    WOMEN
Yes.

LOUISE is on the floor in front of PIN-MAN.

                    ALLAN
What is your name, little girl?

                    LOUISE
Louise.

                    ALLAN
You have been a very naughty girl, Louise.

                    LOUISE
Don't hurt me.

                    ALLAN
I only want to play with you.

                    LOUISE
Don't hurt me.

ALLAN
I only want to play with you.

LOUISE screams.

CREAM
Are you enjoying yourself, Sir Hugh?

ALLAN removes his mask.

ALLAN
You like to have your little games, don't you Doctor? You like to play your little tricks, spying on me for Lord Strathcona?

ALLAN removes his gloves.

CREAM
Sir?

ALLAN
The letters that are missing from my portfolio, Doctor...

CREAM
Letters that proved that Sir Hugh had spent over 400,000 dollars in bribes given to Sir John A. Macdonald and various other members of the Conservative Party.

ALLAN
Who promised that I would be granted the contract to construct the Canadian Pacific Railway.

CREAM
From Coast to Coast.

STRATHCONA
From the Atlantic to the Pacific, Mr. Cream, providing, of course that those letters do not surface in the wrong hands.

CREAM

Letters that Strathcona wants.

ALLAN

Letters that belong to me.

CREAM

Letters that disappeared one of the nights that Henri Joseph Wilfrid Laurier came to the Elite Club.

WOMEN 1, 3

Case Number Four.

CREAM

He was a bit of a strange one. A voyeur, perhaps, although he never went upstairs. No, he would sit in our grand salon taking refreshments, waiting, he said, for a friend. But he never said who.

CAMILLE

A rose in his lapel and the eyes of a poet.

LAURIER

Never have I met anyone as beautiful as you, mademoiselle.

CAMILLE

He said. And he meant it.

CREAM

Laurier always meant what he said when he said it.
That was his charm, that was his grace.

LAURIER

Please understand, mademoiselle.

CAMILLE

He said.

LAURIER

I am not a patron of this house, but I would like the pleasure of a promenade?

LAURIER and CAMILLE hold hands and take a stroll.

CREAM

And Laurier began taking Camille out for walks in the evenings along the fashionable boulevards, first as a friend. Then, ah, how sweet.

LAURIER and CAMILLE kiss.

CREAM

As lovers.

LAURIER and CAMILLE's conversations can be performed en français.

LAURIER

I've told you so much about myself, but you say nothing.

CAMILLE

There is nothing to say,

CREAM

A young patriot and quite a radical in those days was Henri Joseph Wilfrid Laurier, having just started his political career.

LAURIER

I studied Law at McGill University, Camille. I studied English because, well, it was necessary for my advancement. But being there in an institution that boasts of having Sir John Colborne as one of its governors, the butcher who crushed the Rebellion of 1837, made me aware of the utter contempt the Anglophone elite have for our people, Camille. Look at the way we live. Look at me, ashamed of being what I am. A canadien. But no more!

CAMILLE

And Laurier said what I knew in my heart, but he said it to me. He made me see that I was not just another silly young whore.

LAURIER

You are their prize, Camille. You are their privilege.

CAMILLE

And I must not let myself be used in this way.

LAURIER

You must be free.

CAMILLE

Quebec must be free.

LAURIER
(Singing)

But life is real
And so are we

CAMILLE
(Singing)

And still we dream
Of what might be

LAURIER

I am weak
I'm not that strong

CAMILLE

The change will come
It will be done

LAURIER

The words I speak
Were given to me

CAMILLE

You cannot help
What has to be

LAURIER

But if I lose
what will we do?

CAMILLE

We'll call your name
and fight again

LAURIER

My people ask
too much of me

CAMILLE

It's not your choice
It's you we need

LAURIER
(Quoting Byron)
"Eternal spirit of the chainless mind
Brightest in dungeons, liberty thou art
For there thy habitation is the heart
The heart which love of thee alone can bind
And when thy sons to fetters are consigned
To fetters and the damp vaults dayless gloom
Their country conquers with their martyrdom."

*WOMAN TWO transfers into a masculine figure by a simple
change of costume.*

ARMAND

And my sister Camille began giving Laurier most of the
money she made as a prostitute, money that Laurier used
to promote himself.

LAURIER

And the rights of Quebec.

ARMAND

This at a time when two small children froze to death inside
of their house on Young Street in Pointe Saint Charles.

WOMEN 1, 3

Ice on the windows.

ARMAND

Ice on the floor.

WOMEN 1, 3

Cold.

ARMAND

Cold.

WOMEN 1, 3

Cold.

ARMAND

On January the ninth, 1872.

WOMEN 1, 3

In Pointe Saint Charles.

LAURIER

And these children did not just die from the weather, my
friends, oh no. They died from the high prices, low wages
and bad housing that is the result of the Conservative
Party's policy of support for certain capitalists in this
country, who are ready to see the people of Quebec go
down in ruins rather than risk one dollar of their profits.

WOMEN 1, 3

Laurier.

LAURIER

But we plan to put an end to such misery.

WOMEN 1, 3

Oui.

LAURIER

We plan to put an end to such horrors.

WOMEN 1, 3

Oui.

LAURIER

And united behind the Liberal Party's policy of justice and
equality for all, we will see a new Quebec emerge, a strong
Quebec in which our children will not suffer and die, but
live and prosper in a nation free of the kind of exploitation
that led to the deaths of these two children.

Cheers.

ARMAND

But what kind of justice was the Liberal Party talking about?
What kind of freedom? Freedom for what? Freedom for
who? Because you can't have Westmount without Pointe
Saint Charles and you can't have Pointe Saint Charles
without Westmount.

LAURIER

All men of good faith must work together.

ARMAND

You are speaking for yourself, Laurier.

LAURIER

I am speaking for all of us.

ARMAND

And I warned Camille that Laurier was not to be trusted.

CAMILLE

I love him.

ARMAND

He doesn't know who he is.

CAMILLE

I love him.

ARMAND

He will betray you.

LAURIER

I did love her.

CAMILLE

And he gave me a ring, this ring.

GUIDE

Exhibit Number Five

WOMAN 1 & ARMAND

Exhibit Number Five

LAURIER

Leave this place, Camille, come live with me.

CAMILLE

No, you must not think this way.

LAURIER

The Government under pressure from the Church has already closed down my newspaper. My days as a politician are numbered.

CAMILLE

Your people need you, Laurier.

LAURIER

I need you, Camille.

CAMILLE

But I knew what I had to do.

ARMAND

They will find out, Camille.

JOSIE

They will kill you.

ARMAND

They will find out, Camille.

JOSIE

They will kill you.

CAMILLE

I knew what I had to do.

CREAM

I, of course, was aware of Camille's growing support for Laurier's political campaign and I had more sympathy for their cause than they might have supposed. I, who always refused to be judged by the petty, oh so petty, bourgeois. And in my own inimitable way I believe I posed a greater threat to the status quo than any number of Joseph Armands, although my object was not the overthrow of the established order, but my own elevation above it. My purpose and deed not being political, but egotistic in the War of Each against All.

ARMAND

(Selling a socialist newspaper) Journal Socialiste. Support Quebec's right to self-determination. Stop Tory attacks on the workers. Equality for women.

CREAM

Ah yes, the noble proletariat and how are we today? Working hard, I hope? Being busy, aren't we, Joseph? Plans, big plans I hear. Oh, the ruling class is shaking in their very boots at the thought of your upcoming protest. Well timed, I must say, but then, I believe something even more drastic than a simple protest is being seriously considered?

ARMAND

What did he mean?

CREAM

Oh, I hear things, Joseph. Yes I do, and I would like to hear more.

ARMAND

I know nothing of what you are saying and if I did, do you really think I would tell you something?

CREAM

Others do.

ARMAND

Not me.

CREAM

Joseph, you can't win. You are going to lose. I don't even
have to tell you that. You know you are going to lose. So
why not help yourself?

ARMAND

I am not that important.

CREAM

Oh yes, you are, to yourself. You to yourself, I to myself. We
are all alone. Alone. Close your eyes and the stars will
disappear, Joseph.

CREAM exiting. Mockingly:

"So I tell you, all good sailormen
Tak' warning by dat storm
An' go an' marry some nice French girl
An' leav on wan beeg farm
De win' can blow lak' hurricane
An' s'pose she blow some more
You can't get drown on Lac St. Pierre
So long you stay on shore."

ARMAND

We will win.

LAURIER

I was in my chambers at the Ottawa Hotel on Rue Saint
Jacques, sitting by the window, wondering what to do.
Return to my former life in Arthabaska? Was that all I was
capable of doing? I, who had been the favourite of my
mother, the darling of the village priest, the first in my

class, loved by my people and now, with all my high ambitions, could I resign myself to being second rate?

CAMILLE
(Gives letters to LAURIER) Laurier.

LAURIER
I was stunned, shocked by what I read.

CAMILLE
We have them now, Laurier.

LAURIER
No, you don't understand, Camille, I cannot use these letters. I cannot publish them because of the effect that this information would have on the people of Quebec. It would only strengthen those who advocate the violent overthrow of our society.

CAMILLE
Laurier.

LAURIER
What would you have me do? Ally myself with the Anarchists, the Socialists, like your brother Joseph Armand, who speaks of the future as a wonderful place of peace and plenty? Yes, they have a fine vision, but, in truth they will only bring death upon us. Death and the end of any sense or need of loyalty, friendship and love. They never use that word, Camille, that word, love.

CAMILLE
What are you going to do, Laurier?

LAURIER
I don't know.

CREAM
But I knew.

ALLAN

A magnificent view, isn't it, Mr. Laurier? I often come up here in the morning to watch my ships come in. North-South-East-West. "The Sarmitan" from Liverpool, "The Parthian" due out for Copenhagen, and there, taking the shallow near Ile de Ronde, our latest, "The African," equipped with new rotary propellers which enable her to travel at a constant speed of eleven knots per hour. Speed and efficiency, that's what I built this company on, sir, beginning with a single lumber barge over forty years ago, to one of the world's largest shipping companies. An achievement, monsieur, that I can justly feel proud of, don't you think?

LAURIER

Surely, sir.

ALLAN

Asia, Africa, Malaysia, the East Indies, it's all there for the taking. Just waiting to be used and properly exploited.

LAURIER

For your profit, sir.

ALLAN

For my profit.

LAURIER

And what gives you the right?

ALLAN

I do not demand any rights, monsieur, nor do I recognize any. What I can get by force, I get by force. What I can't get, I have no right to.

LAURIER

I am not sure what you mean, sir.

ALLAN

I think you know what I mean, monsieur, otherwise you would not be here.

LAURIER

I am here, sir, to return your property.

ALLAN

You are here, monsieur, because you finally realized that
you will never be who you want to be unless I say so.
Otherwise you will return from whence you came, sir,
another obscure lawyer in yet another small town. Only
you, sir will have the bitter knowledge of what might have
been.

LAURIER

My people love me, sir.

ALLAN

The people have a short memory, sir. They forget
everything and they will forget you too. And I think you
want to be remembered. I think you want to be the next Sir
George Etienne Cartier.

LAURIER

I would not presume, sir, to be worthy of such an honour.

ALLAN

Cartier? Worthy of being Cartier? I made that creature. He
belongs to me just like the rest of the politicians in this
province and I can make you too, Laurier. But there is price
to pay, monsieur. There is always a price to pay.

LAURIER

Camille.

ALLAN

Yes.

LAURIER

She knows nothing. She doesn't understand those letters.

ALLAN

But you do, Laurier, and if word should get out about this
affair to the Governor General?

LAURIER

I can guarantee their silence.

ALLAN

And yours?

LAURIER

You have my word.

ALLAN

You know what they say about politicians, monsieur. When they talk, they're lying. When they're quiet, they're stealing.

LAURIER

I swear on my honour as a gentleman that I will never speak or move against you on the issue of the Canadian Pacific Railway.

ALLAN

Lord Dufferin will be arriving in Montreal this week, Laurier. She must die.

LAURIER

No.

ALLAN

She must die.

LAURIER

No, you cannot speak to me this way, Sir Hugh, as if were discussing the elimination of a plus or minus point from one of your business ledgers. We are talking about a person, a young woman. The woman I love.

ALLAN

Good day, monsieur.

LAURIER

I love her.

ALLAN

Good day.

LAURIER

I did love her.

CREAM

Love—love—love. A word for all seasons. When everything
else fails, tell her that you love her, tell her that you need
her, tell her that she is the only one for you—Blue Moon—
but don't forget to carry a big stick.

LAURIER

Camille.

THE DEAD circle around CREAM wearing masquerade masks.

CREAM

Gentlemen, as members of the Elite Club, you have
regularly partaken of all manner of sin and temptation of
this house, participating with these ladies in a wide rage of
sexual experimentation, each one a little more on the edge
of the conclusion that we have reached this evening on this,
the final closing night of our Club. Oh yes, dear, good loyal
and faithful servants, it is only too true that each and every
one of you will indeed disappear, vanish as if you had never
existed, along with this house and all of its history, for
reasons, well, far beyond my control and your
comprehension. So let us, then, dear ladies, accept our sad
situation with as much grace as possible and end our last
moments together, not in whines or whimpers, but in the
sweet ecstasy of that ultimate fantasy.

THE DEAD

Death.

CREAM

I am going to kill you.

THE DEAD

Yoohoo Louise.

CREAM

Louise, yoohoo.

THE DEAD

I'm going to kill you.

CREAM

Oh, she don't speak the h'english.

LOUISE giggles and skips around.

CREAM

Peek-a-boo.

THE DEAD

I see you.

CREAM

Peek-a-boo.

THE DEAD

I see you.

CREAM

Parlez-parlez-parlez-vous.

CAMILLE

And she was laughing. She thought he was joking.

THE DEAD

You are going to die.

CREAM

You silly little bitch.

THE DEAD

You are going to die.

CAMILLE

And he put her scarf around her neck.

THE DEAD

Surprise.

CREAM

Surprise.

THE DEAD

Surprise.

CREAM

Oh, she looks scared now.

CAMILLE

And pulled and pulled and pulled.

CREAM
(Sings)
Jesus loves me this I know
For the Bible tells me so.

LOUISE

Uh.

CREAM pulls the scarf away from her neck.

CREAM

She pee-peed herself.

THE DEAD

She pee-peed herself.

CREAM

Pee-pee.

THE DEAD

Ca-ca.

CREAM

Pee-pee.

THE DEAD

Ca-ca.

CREAM

Shame.

THE DEAD

Shame.

CREAM

Shame.

THE DEAD

She pee-peed herself.

CREAM

Little ones to him belong
They are weak, but he is strong.

THE DEAD

Josie.

CREAM

Yoohoo, Josie.

THE DEAD

Josie, you hoo.

CREAM

I'm going to kill you.

JOSIE runs to the back.

JOSIE

It wasn't me.

CREAM

Oh, it wasn't you.

JOSIE

(Points to CAMILLE) She made me do it.

CREAM

Oh, she made her do it.

THE DEAD

Oh.

CREAM

Oh.

CAMILLE

And she crawled into a corner.

JOSIE

Please.

CAMILLE

She said.

JOSIE

Please.

CREAM

I'm going to kill you.

CAMILLE

And he kicked.

CREAM

And kicked.

THE DEAD

And kicked and kicked and kicked!

JOSIE collapses. CREAM drags her by the heels to the middle of the floor, next to LOUISE.

CREAM
(Singing)

Yes, Jesus loves me
Yes, Jesus loves me
Yes, Jesus loves me
The Bible tells me so.

THE DEAD

Camille.

CREAM

Yoohoo, Camille.

GUIDE

"How Low Can You Go."

CREAM
(Singing)

A knock on the door
But who is it for
You say to yourself
It's somebody else
Please, no
Is it really my time to go
Say it's not so
A sudden quick moan
With a cut to the bone

Chorus:

THE DEAD

Just a minute more
Just a minute more
Just a minute more

CREAM

How low can you go
How low can you go
How low can you go

Chorus ends.

CREAM

You never can tell
'till the moment is felt
the feeling of pain
that comes back again
but no it really is time to go
I must say it is so
I'll tell you no lies
You are going to die

Chorus:

THE DEAD

Just a minute more
Just a minute more
Just a minute more

CREAM

How low can you go
How low can you go
How low can you go
I want to kill someone
I want to kill someone
want to kill someone
I want to kill someone
I want to kill, I want to kill
I want to kill, kill, kill, kill,
kill, kill, kill, kill, kill, kill,
kill, kill, kill

Chorus ends.

CREAM

Long lonely nights
Long lonely days
All a bad dream
As you hear yourself scream
Oh no In the mirror you see it is so
I'm the one that you know
Good-bye my dear friend
I'll see you again

Chorus:

THE DEAD

Just a minute more
Just a minute more
Just a minute more

CREAM

How low can you go
How low can you go
How low can you go
I want to kill someone
I want to kill someone
I want to kill someone
I want to kill someone
I want to kill, I want to kill
I want to kill

THE DEAD

Kill

CREAM

Kill

THE DEAD

Kill

CREAM

Kill

90

	THE DEAD
Kill	
	CREAM
Kill	
	THE DEAD
Kill	
	CREAM
Kill	
	THE DEAD
Kill	
	CREAM
Kill	
	THE DEAD
Kill	
	CREAM
Kill	
	THE DEAD
Kill	
	CREAM
Kill	
	THE DEAD
Kill	
	CREAM
Kill	

Chorus ends.

THE DEAD

She's gone?

CREAM

She's gone?

THE DEAD

She's gone.

ALLAN takes of his mask.

ALLAN

You must find her, Cream.

CREAM

Find her.

THE DEAD

You must find her, Cream.

CREAM

Find her.

STRATHCONA

Look at you, Mr. Cream. Look at me.

CREAM

(Turns around to face STRATHCONA) I did not know I could feel like this.

STRATHCONA

You must not let yourself be overwhelmed by the taste of the kill, Mr. Cream. Not now—I need you.

CREAM sighs and shivers.

STRATHCONA

Do you remember what I told you about power? How it could destroy you? Listen carefully: You will find those letters and you will give them to me, not to Sir Hugh.

CREAM

And what was he really saying and how much did he really know?

STRATHCONA

Do not insult our intelligence by even attempting to deny whatever counter-proposal you may have accepted from Sir Hugh Allan, Mr. Cream. Just remember what I told you and have faith in what I say. Sir Hugh is not destined to have the Canadian Pacific Railway. It will be mine.

WOMEN 1, 2

"Engine, engine Number Nine
Going down Chicago line
If the train falls off the track
Do you want your money back?"

ALLAN

Yes.

WOMAN 1

Y *(points at STRATHCONA)*

WOMAN 2

E *(points at ALLAN)*

WOMAN 1

S *(points at STRATHCONA)*

WOMAN 2

Spells *(points at ALLAN)*

WOMAN 1

Yes *(points at STRATHCONA)*

WOMAN 2

And *(points at ALLAN)*

WOMAN 1

You *(points at STRATHCONA)*

WOMAN 2

Are *(points at ALLAN)*

WOMAN 1

Not (*points at* STRATHCONA)

WOMAN 2

It. (*points at* ALLAN)

ARMAND

Now as we look back, it seems inevitable that the history of Quebec would evolve the way it has. Our industries and resources being developed by the Anglophone elite of Montreal for their benefit and profit. But the moment was there for us to seize—it is here now, comrades. But where is Laurier?

DUFFERIN enters, carrying a Union Jack flag.

DUFFERIN

A Mari Usque Ad Mare.

THE DEAD

A Mari Usque Ad Mare.

DUFFERIN

O Lord God Almighty.

THE DEAD

O Lord God Almighty.

DUFFERIN

Who rulest nations of the Earth, we humbly beseech Thee with Thy favour to behold Our Sovereign Lady, Queen Victoria, that in all things she may be led by Thy guidance.

THE DEAD

And protected by Thy power.

DUFFERIN

"God of our fathers, known of old
Lord of the far flung battle line

Beneath whose awful hand we hold
Dominion over palm and pine
Lord God of hosts, be with us yet
Lest we forget."

THE DEAD
Lest We Forget.

ARMAND
I was arrested that night, picked up off the street, along
with twenty other comrades, the leaders of the protest we
had planned for the next day in front of McGill University
where Lord Dufferin was scheduled to dedicate a new
Science Building. I could hear cheers inside of my prison
cell. We had lost. This time.

THE DEAD
And forever and ever.

DUFFERIN
Let it remembered that we laboured to further the cause of
peace and prosperity, in our service to others.

THE DEAD
Noblesse oblige

CREAM
Following the dedication, Lord Dufferin and his entourage
proceeded towards Ravenscrag, the house of Sir Hugh
Allan, located on the very highest edge of the mountain,
overlooking the whole city.

ALLAN
My city.

CREAM
Where Lord Dufferin was to be wined and dined at a
banquet that had cost Sir Hugh thirty thousand dollars.

ALLAN

I awaited Lord Dufferin, Her Majesty's Representative in Canada, at my home, to welcome him, according to proper protocol, as the host. It was to be my crowning moment.

CREAM

The carriage ride, up Beaver Hall Hill in the slanting sun of a long golden afternoon. The radiant candor of His Lordship's gaze, the sense of poise as he turns his Imperial eyes westward towards the Pacific.

DUFFERIN

Vancouver.

CREAM

Hong Kong.

DUFFERIN

Singapore.

CREAM

Rangoon.

DUFFERIN

Calcutta.

CREAM

Johannesburg.

DUFFERIN

Montreal.

CREAM

With the hum of the great world echoing in his ears.

DUFFERIN

The ruling class.

CREAM

Masters of the earth and sea.

THE DEAD

Lest We Forget.

CREAM

And Sir Hugh's private orchestra began to play as the Governor General and other guests entered the glittering mansion, shining, sparkling, smiling in the light.

WOMEN 1, 3

Their light.

ARMAND

Their mountain.

WOMEN 1, 3

Their city.

ARMAND

Their world.

WOMAN 1, 3

Assassins.

ARMAND

Assassins.

WOMEN 1, 3

Assassins.

ARMAND

"Je suis le chien qui ronge l'os."

WOMEN 1, 3

"En le rongeant, je prends mon repos."

ARMAND

"Un jour viendra qui n'est pas venu."

ARMAND & WOMEN 1, 3

"Ou je mordrai qui m'aura mordu."

LAURIER points at LORD DUFFERIN.

LAURIER

And I raised my gun.

WOMEN & ARMAND

Shoot him.

LAURIER

But it makes no difference.

WOMEN & ARMAND

Shoot him.

LAURIER

But they've already won.

WOMEN & ARMAND

Shoot him.

LAURIER

They've already won. *(LAURIER lowers his arm.)*

DUFFERIN

Gentlemen, there is no doubt in my mind that a railway link from Halifax to Vancouver and from hence to Asia is absolutely vital in terms of a global military strategy, designed to confront the growing expansion of Germany, the United States and indeed, Japan, into British spheres of influence. And the logical choice of heading such a momentous undertaking, gentlemen, by rank and seniority is you, Sir Hugh Allan. But that will not happen, gentlemen. Not because of bribing government officials, because after all, someone has to bribe them. *(giggles)* Not even the fact that you have been using American money, Sir Hugh?

ALLAN

I have broken off those contracts, my Lord.

DUFFERIN

We knew you would, sir. But then there is a little matter of your fascination with pins.

ALLAN

We all have our fascinations, isn't that correct, Lord Strathcona?

DUFFERIN

Yes, and the question whether such behavior is reprehensible is inconsequential in the eyes of the State. What I think personally is inconsequential, but, such facts have a tendency to surface, Sir Hugh, and Laurier does not know about Nati Mascou, but he knows about Camille Armand. And here we have our main point in discussion. Cartier is dying, gentlemen, and the call for an independent Quebec is again being heard in the province, a voice that must not be crushed as it was in 1837, but contained. And the man for that is Laurier.

ALLAN

There are other patriots available, sir, for the position of Premier in this province.

DUFFERIN

But none of them have the credibility of Laurier, Sir Hugh. And we must have him if British hegemony over Quebec and Canada is to be maintained at this crucial moment, at a minimum of expense.

ALLAN

But my investments? I have spent a great deal of money, my Lord.

DUFFERIN

And you will be rewarded in due time. But you must not make trouble for us on this issue, sir Hugh. You must not push this point any further, if you value your credit rating on Lombard Street.

ALLAN

My Lord.

DUFFERIN

And finally there is the question of Camille Armand.

STRATHCONA

She has been located, my Lord.

DUFFERIN

And Laurier understands.

LAURIER

Yes.

CAMILLE

Dulce et Decorum est Pro Patria Mori (Honour those who died for their country).

WOMEN 1, 2

Dulce et Decorum est Pro Patria Mori.

CAMILLE

Dulce.

WOMEN 1, 2

Dulce.

CAMILLE

Dulce.

CREAM

She was praying in the Cathedral at the altar after the last Mass. The candles were burning, the incense. No moon outside.

WOMAN 1

In November.

WOMAN 2

In the rain.

WOMAN 1

In the wind.

CREAM

Laurier came in and knelt down beside her. She looked
sad, she looked tired.

LAURIER

Pray for the executioners, pray for the victims, pray for me,
Camille.

CAMILLE

Am I going to die, Laurier?

LAURIER

Yes.

CAMILLE

Am I going to die?

DUFFERIN

We are but slaves of destiny and fate, gentlemen. We do
what we must, not what we will, if civilization is to be
protected against our own natures and the dark forces that
now threaten to pull down our empire.

THE DEAD

Lest We Forget.

GUIDE

Exhibit Number Six.

WOMEN 1, 2

Exhibit Number Six.

GUIDE
A one-inch-thick, ten-inch-long spike of Bessemer steel,
presented to Lord Strathcona by the representative in
Canada of Her Royal Britannic Majesty.

WOMEN 1, 2
"The Last Spike."

STRATHCONA
Arise and come to your God.

CREAM
Laurier took Camille by the hand.

STRATHCONA
Arise and come to your God.

CREAM
He led her outside on the steps.

THE DEAD
Arise.

CREAM
I grabbed her by the hair.

WOMAN 1
In the wind.

WOMAN 2
In the rain.

LAURIER
Make it quick.

THE DEAD
Make it fast.

CREAM
She turned around.

LAURIER

Make it quick.

THE DEAD

Make it fast.

CREAM

Strathcona raised the Last Spike.

LAURIER

Make it quick.

THE DEAD

Make it fast.

LAURIER

Make it quick.

THE DEAD

Make it fast.

STRATHCONA lowers the spike and CAMILLE bows her head in death.

WOMEN 1, 2

O sisters.

LAURIER

And my record is clear. A good record of reform in education here in Quebec, where I helped outlaw child labour and limit the work day to ten hours. But yes, I had to give up on my ideals. I learnt to fight only for what is possible and became a pragmatist like your monsieur Trudeau, holding the utopian dreams of my youth in utter contempt...but, in my heart, dans mon coeur, I knew, I knew.

WOMAN 2

And he became a thing in the eyes of the world.

WOMEN 1, 3

A statue in Dominion Square.

WOMAN 2

A face on the five-dollar bill.

WOMEN 1, 3

An image.

WOMAN 2

A token.

WOMEN 1, 3

A cliché.

LAURIER

And nothing to myself.

WOMEN

Lost.

LAURIER

Lost.

WOMEN

Lost.

CAMILLE
(Quoting from a poem by Emile Nelligan)
"Ce fut un Vasseur d'or dont les flans diaphanes

WOMEN 1, 2

Revelaient des trésors que les marins profanes

CAMILLE

Dégoût, Haine, et Névrose, entre eux disputé

WOMEN 1, 2

Que reste-il de lui dans la tempête brave?

CAMILLE

Qu'est devenu mon coeur deserté?

CAMILLE & WOMEN 1, 2

Hélas, il a sombré dans l'abîme du Rêve."

LAURIER

Camille.

GUIDE

Exhibit Number Seven.

WOMEN 1, 3

Exhibit Number Seven.

GUIDE

The skull of a young female, aged sixteen.

CREAM proceeds to examine the skull.

CREAM

Mandible loose and fractured with the temporo-manibular ligament still intact. Frontal. Parietal, temporal and sphenoid bones complete but minus your hair and your eyes and your lips—alas, poor Camille, where are the charms of yesteryear?

WOMEN

Remember.

CREAM strikes a match.

CREAM

The Elite Club burnt down to the ground the night that Doctor Thomas Neill Cream left Montreal for an extended pleasure tour of the United States. Lord Strathcona led him to believe that he would be rewarded in due time for services rendered, but, of course they had to get rid of me.

WOMEN

Now that the deed is done
Now that the race is won

CREAM

And it happened in England, London, England, in the very heart of the British Empire where I was charged and sentenced to death for the murder of a prostitute. Nothing serious, you understand, just for fun. A bit of amusement.

WOMEN

Listen.

CREAM

The last meal ordered out from a French restaurant, along with a bottle of Beaujolais rouge, lifting my glass in a toast. "Gentlemen scholars out on a spree, damned to Eternity."

WOMEN

Listen.

CREAM

Twelve o'clock, twelve o'clock midnight, on the stroke of twelve, the sound of the steel doors slamming and the echo of footsteps along the stone corridor.

WOMEN

Are you ready, Doctor Cream?

CREAM

The gentlemen of the Press and other official witnesses were there when I entered, standing in the shadow of the gallows as I saluted them. "I hope you will enjoy my last performance, my final bow."

WOMEN

Listen.

CREAM

The weight of the rope, the smell of the hemp, a sudden pull.

WOMEN

Any last words?

CREAM

And I smiled.

WOMEN

Any last words?

CREAM

I smiled as my body slipped and slapped into the noose, snapping down into the darkness. Twitching and turning, turning and twitching.

WOMEN

Turning.

CREAM

Twitching.

WOMEN

Turning.

CREAM

Death by strangulation, caused by the dislocation of various cervical vertebrae. A legal execution, all very, very legal and well-orchestrated by certain people in high places who condemned me as an infamous creature. A vicious ingrate, as if any of my silly little games could in any way compare to the World War that broke out only eight months after Lord Strathcona died. A war in which millions died, butchered and slaughtered by the very science and education that these gentlemen were supposedly developing in the interests and advancement of humanity. But still I said nothing. I would not even give my name because I knew there would yet be another rendezvous when I would stand acknowledged and revealed—as the true school spirit of McGill.

WOMEN
As long as you believe.

WOMEN
"Jack the Ripper's dead
And lying in his bed
We cut his throat with Sunlight soap
Jack the Ripper's dead."

THE DEAD and CREAM drift off into their original places.

CREAM
(Singing to the tune of "Believe Me If All Those Endearing Young Charms")
So hail Alma Mater, thy shades and thy halls
It's been nice to behold them once more
To revisit old scenes, feel the warm grasp of hands
Of the comrades our hearts loved of yore
Farewell, be thy destinies onward and bright
Our fond hearts shall follow thee still
May thy sons and thy daughters all cherish and love
Forever the name of McGill.

CREAM goes back in his tomb.

WOMEN
(To audience) Kill them.

Lights fade. Then WOMAN TWO along with WOMAN ONE and THREE take centre positions.

GUIDE
Comrades and friends, we will now recess in order to consider the evidence against the illustrious dead of McGill, who now stand charged with the murder of Nati Mascou and Camille Armand. After further discussion we will reach a verdict by voting—

WOMEN
(Together) —Guilty or Not Guilty.

WOMEN exit.

During the intermission, the audience will be presented with the historical facts the play is based upon, centring around the oppression and exploitation of the Native and Quebecois people by the Anglophone elite of Montreal and the Canadian Pacific Railway Scandal of 1872-73. When the audience returns to its seats, the cast members—out of costume—will be ready to debate the questions raised in the script and discuss their own opinions on the historical characters they have portrayed.

HISTORICAL APPENDIX

Doctor Thomas Neill Cream was born in Glasgow, Scotland, on May 27, 1850. His family immigrated to Quebec, in 1854 or 1855, where his father became a wholesale lumber merchant. Thomas, the eldest son, worked in the family business for a while but in October 1872, at the age of twenty-two, he registered as a student of Medicine at McGill University.

It is said that he gained a reputation as being rather flamboyant while training as an intern in the University Lying-In Hospital—a Charity Hospital for the Poor and Destitute, located on Rue Saint Dominique in the heart of Montreal's red light district. But despite youthful indulgences, Cream managed to graduate with merit and received his M.D. diploma on March 31, 1876. The address delivered to the graduates by the Dean of the Faculty was entitled "The Evils of Malpractice in the Medical Profession."

One of Cream's lecturers in Medicine at McGill was William Featherstone Osler, who was only a year older than Cream and already well on his way to international fame as a diagnostician and foremost pathologist. He taught Cream how to perform autopsies, most of them on working-class people who had died prematurely as a consequence of poverty. The statistics tell the story: In 1895, the death rate in the "City Above the Hill"—in Westmount where the Anglophone elite lived—was less that 13 per 1,000; in Saint Gabriel's Ward, the "City Below the Hill," it was 32.32%. The exceptionally high rate of mortality was blamed on unsanitary conditions, impure water, tainted milk and the ignorance of the workers themselves—particularly the Francophones who, at one point, rioted because they were afraid to be vaccinated for smallpox. But it was the Anglophone elite that benefitted from all that misery. Poor

111

housing, unsanitary conditions and inadequate wages translated into big profits for the tiny minority living in Westmount, who owned and controlled over half of the wealth in Canada.

Cream, as a member of this elite, never questioned its right to rule or the consequences of its governing. Like the majority of his class, he simply acccptcd the life around him as a given fact. The poor were poor but that was not his problem—he had a career to consider. However, shortly after his graduation, Cream committed an act that put him beyond the pale: He got a woman from a respectable family pregnant, then procured her an abortion which made her very ill. The family discovered what had happened and forced Cream, literally by shot-gun, to marry Miss Flora Eliza Brooks of Waterloo, Quebec. The day after the wedding, Cream left the house for England to complete his medical training, the ensuing scandal having ruined his chances of setting up a practice in Montreal.

After gaining his honours as a post-graduate student in Edinburgh, Scotland, Cream returned to Canada and set up practice in London, Ontario. During his residence there, the mysterious death of a young woman named Kate Gardener, a chambermaid in a hotel, caused a considerable stir. The body of the woman, bottle of chloroform by her side, was found in a privy behind the premises occupied by Cream. At the adjourned inquest, it came out that the girl had been frequenting Cream's office in order to get an abortion. The evidence pointed plainly to murder instead of suicide, several doctors swearing to the impossibility of the woman chloroforming herself given the state in which she was found. The verdict returned was: "The deceased died from Chloroform, administered by some person unknown." But suspicion against Cream was so strong that he was forced to leave London, and shortly afterwards left for the United States.

In Chicago, Cream soon earned a very unsavoury reputation as a back-street abortionist and in the early part of the following year, 1881, he became involved in a scheme that landed him in jail. Cream had been advertising a remedy for epilepsy in a Chicago newspaper. Daniel Stott, who lived in the suburbs, sent his wife to visit Cream in order to procure the remedy. Stott was sixty-one, his wife only thirty-three. Julia Stott became Cream's mistress over the course of her frequent visits to Chicago to obtain fresh supplies of medicine for her husband. Cream convinced Mrs. Stott to coax her husband into taking out life insurance, then gave her a prescription full of strychnine to give to him. He died, and Cream was found guilty of murder in the second degree. Subsequently, he was sentenced to life imprisonment in the Illinois State Penitentiary at Joliet.

The bribing of prison officials in order to procure a pardon was common practice in those days, and in 1891 Cream's life sentence was commuted by the Governor of Illinois to one of seventeen years. Cream returned to Montreal for a brief visit with his family and then booked a berth on an Allan steamship for England. In London during the autumn of 1892, Cream proceeded to poison a series of prostitutes just for the fun of it. He was caught and sentenced to death. Some accounts state that on the day of his hanging, as he was dropping through the trap, he yelled: "I am Jack the Ripper." Don Bell, a Montreal writer, has tried to prove in a series of articles that Cream and the Ripper were one and the same person. His theories are interesting—but whether Cream was the world's most famous killer is not what concerns me as a playwright. I am trying to prove that Cream was indeed the true school spirit of McGill University.

Were the "Illustrious Dead" of McGill University—Sir William Osler, Lord Strathcona, Sir Hugh Allan and Sir Wilfrid Laurier—guilty of murder as charged in the play? Yes and no. Yes—if one considers the "Illustrious Dead" of McGill as part of a ruling elite directly responsible for the gross exploitation and oppression of the Quebecois and

Native peoples of Quebec, an oppression that led to thousands of premature deaths. No—if one sticks only to a legal definition of the act of murder by an individual. In either case, my purpose in bringing Doctor Cream back to life is to demonstrate that the "Illustrious Dead" were exploiters, not benefactors; opportunists, not philanthropists. They were criminal in their general intentions. This hidden history can best be brought out by a detailed account of the careers of two men whose names are honoured by McGill: Sir Hugh Allan and Lord Strathcona.

Sir Hugh Allan, described in the National Biography as "one of Canada's first monopoly capitalists," first came to Montreal in 1826, at the age of sixteen. As a scion of a powerful Scottish shipping family, he rapidly became one of the central figures in the transformation of Montreal from a fairly insignificant provincial town into an international seaport. Never one to miss out on a lucrative opportunity, Allan made a killing during the 1840s when famine in Ireland forced millions of starving Irish to emigrate. Allan used the emigrants as ballast in lumber ships that would have otherwise returned empty from Europe. However, the ships were designed to carry lumber, not human beings, and an average of one out of every three passengers did not survive the voyage across the Atlantic. When a newspaper, the *Montreal Witness*, dared to criticize the company, Allan sued for libel. He lost the case.

By the 1860s, the Allan Steamship Line was the largest merchant fleet sailing the North Atlantic, with weekly departures for Liverpool and Glasgow from Montreal. Having won dominance over the Saint Lawrence River Valley shipping lines, Allan then began to consider railways: He was vulnerable in that area because his steamships were dependent on railway head deliveries. Thus, he welcomed the idea of a new transcontinental railway to be built by private enterprise with government subsidies. He then proceeded to determine that the contract would be awarded to him. Sir John A. Macdonald, who owed Allan $80,000, virtually promised Allan the contract to construct the Pacific Railway, but Lucius Seth Huntington stood up in Parliament and charged Allan with bribery. He stated that the Conservative Party had agreed to award Allan the contract in return for the payment of certain funds—some coming from American sources. Macdonald, then Prime Minister of Canada, denied it all. But when Allan's correspondence with his American financial backers and political allies were published, he was forced to retreat. Included amongst the correspondence was a telegram from Sir John to Allan's confidential lawyer, stating: "I must have another ten thousand; will be the last time of calling; do not fail me; answer today."

One wonders what would have happened to Canada if Allan had received the contract. Alberta, Manitoba and Saskatchewan would probably have gone to the Americans, and Allan would have controlled the world's largest transportation system. They might have named what was left of Canada "Allania,' after the completion of the railway. But it was not Allan who hammered in "The Last Spike." It was Lord Strathcona.

Strathcona was born Donald A. Smith in 1820, in Forres, Scotland—the district in which Shakespeare had Macbeth and Banquo meet the Weird Sisters. Influenced by his uncle, an officer in the Hudson's Bay Company, at the age of eighteen he emigrated to Canada to become a fur trader. For thirteen years Strathcona traded in Labrador with the Innu, as they call themselves (or the Naskapi, as they are called by others). During those years he prided himself on having the numbers always on the right side of the ledger—in the black, not the red. He was called Manitoupeewa-nisque, "Man of Iron Spirit," by the Innu. He took the name as a compliment, but the Innu did not mean it as such. They meant that he was a man without a heart, one who refused to give them any credit and who let them starve whenever the hunting went bad.

"Because the Hudson's Bay Company controlled the supply of ammunition," said Dr. Alan Cooke of the Hochelaga Institute, "the Nascapi were obliged to spend part of their time trapping furs, mainly marten, whether or not they preferred to hunt caribou. When they abandoned their traditional techniques of hunting caribou for the new technology of guns and ammunition, they gave themselves into the trader's hands. There was no return."

Nine-tenths of the Native population of Labrador died during Strathcona's control over the region in the 1850s, as a consequence of his drive for profit. He returned to Montreal in 1869 as Chief Factor of the Hudson's Bay Company, leaving behind a wilderness depopulated by disease and famine. There he allied himself with his cousin, George Stephen, an executive in the Bank of Montreal. Together they gained control over that financial institution and used it as their private piggy bank, taking out large sums and investing without consent or knowledge of the bank directors. By these illegal means, they were able to purchase the St. Paul and Minneapolis Railway, which links the American mid-west with Manitoba. After this, Strathcona proceeded to wine and dine the Liberal party in order to get his hands on the contract to construct the Canadian Pacific Railway.

When the Liberals, under Mackenzie, failed to come across with the contract, Strathcona began manoeuvring the Conservatives again. He let it be known through his lawyer that money would be available to help secure Sir John A.'s return to power in the pending election—if he would consider favourably a proposal for the construction of the Canadian Pacific Railway by a responsible company. Sir John A. agreed, won the election, and the new Canadian Pacific Railway Syndicate was granted its charter on October 21, 1880.

According to W.R.T. Preston, it was "the most stupendous contract ever made under responsible government in the history of the world." To complete the transcontinental railway in ten years, the Syndicate was granted $206,000,000 in cash, subsidies and stock guarantees, in addition to 25,000,000 acres in land grants. When all the tax benefits and values of the land exchanges are taken in to account, the CPR received gifts from the country worth $106,300,000. The generosity shown towards the Syndicate was helped along by what the CPR directors referred to as "bonifications"—bribery in the form of CPR share options deposited in secret bank accounts. Soon it became hard to tell where the CPR stopped and the government began, the two had become so intertwined— with the CPR directors calling the shots.

Sir Wilfrid Laurier, a Liberal who was elected Prime Minister of Canada in 1895, won on a platform that called for an end to the corruption of the parliamentary system by syndicates like the CPR. But like so many reformers before him and since, Laurier found himself having to compromise with the powers that be. Soon his relationship with the power elite was almost as cordial as the Conservatives' had been. However, Laurier's support for the construction of another transcontinental railway, that might cut into CPR earnings, had Strathcona speak out publicly against him. He was defeated and Robert Laird Borden, a staunch British Imperialist, was elected Prime Minister. One of Borden's first decisions was to order the construction of three battleships as Canada's contribution to the Royal Navy. Great Britain was preparing for war with Germany. The armaments race was on.

Over three hundred McGill students were among the millions who died in World War One, including Sir William Osler's only son. Most of them died believing that they were fighting to defend "Freedom and Democracy." In actuality, they were being slaughtered because of the imperialist ambitions of various ruling elites around the world who were defending their privileges and profits. How could anything Cream did compare to this horror? As William Bolitho said in his book, *Murder for Profit*: "In the neighborhood of a world war, the mass murderer loses all claim to the wholesale and becomes an infinitesimal wretch, engaged in minute wickedness unworthy of attention. So at the trial no lawyer dared to say that the prisoner made him shudder, or to lift the trial and condemnation of a man who had killed a mere handful, out of a class of mere distractions."

Cream was not a chance abnormality. He was a fairly typical product of his time and society. A close study of how the illustrious benefactors of McGill made their fortunes would reveal their involvement in further criminal activities, including bribery, fraud, graft, arson, forgery and, in some cases, murder in the first, second and third degrees. But no ruling class in history has ever come out and said that their rule is based on the oppression and criminal exploitation of the masses. They must justify their existence not only to the ruled, but to themselves. The middle class, in particular, is compelled to put on a show of great concern for the public good because they prefer to rule by consent, through a political democracy. It is simply less expensive if the exploited voluntarily agree to be exploited, rather than admit to open repression. That is why the bourgeoisie are always going on and on about having the interests of the masses at heart. Under pressure they will point to universities such as McGill as bastions of their progressive aims and good intentions.

McGill University is supposed to be a free institution dedicated to rational discourse and freedom of thought, operating without bias or favour. That is not true. McGill is a necessary and central institution of the capitalist social order. It produces technocrats and technicians. It produces ideologies and apologies for class oppression. Its so-called autonomy can be withdrawn at any time by its funding powers. Nor is McGill tolerant of dissent. The university has a long history of dismissing or expelling politically incorrect students and faculty whose worldviews differ from those of the funding powers. The purge and expulsion of Professors Gray, Dixon and Rice are recent examples of that intolerance.

McGill also claims that its mission is to develop science and education in the interests of the whole of humanity—but in reality, it is the multinational corporations that usually benefit from most of the research. Napalm, used extensively during the Vietnam War, was first developed at McGill by Dow Chemical. It has been calculated that the cost of that War—which resulted in the deaths of 2,000,000 Vietnamese and 55,000 Americans—divided among the Vietnamese people could have supplied every peasant with a house, a tractor and thirty acres of land. Instead, Dow Chemical made a profit with every village burnt down by napalm.

Another connection McGill had with American Imperialism was the CIA-funded brainwashing experiments, directed by Doctor Ewan Cameron, Head of McGill's Psychiatric Department at the Allan Memorial Hospital. With the use of various drugs, and sensory deprivation, Cameron would break down patients' personalities, blank out their minds and, with taped messages, try to implant "good thoughts"—approved by the CIA—in their brains. He referred to the process as "psychic overdriving." The patients themselves called it torture. Some of them are now currently suing the CIA and the American government for reparations for the damage done to their lives.

My own connection with McGill first occurred back in the Fifties when my older sister took me and a younger sister up to see the dinosaurs in the Redpath Museum. Walking up from Sherbrooke Street through the Roddick Gates, I saw a strange animal, a rat with a bushy tail. My older sister told me it was a squirrel. I had never seen one. There were not very many trees where I grew up on the avenues in Verdun, and we didn't come uptown that often, because it was not our part of town. When we did go around places like McGill, we had to be very polite and make sure we didn't do or say anything wrong.

I had a dread of the museum. I froze at the sight of all those stuffed animals with eyes that looked hurt and angry about being stitched up in the middle. I refused to walk by the gorilla and I had nightmares about that skeleton behind the glass cabinet for years. Who was that person? Why was his body in a museum? Wouldn't he or she feel bad about that? Imagine if it happened to me? How would I feel about being a skeleton hanging from a rod? Looking at it gave me the lasting impression that McGill University doesn't like animals or people unless they're dead.

Being an Anglophone in Quebec can put you in a death trap if you are unwilling or unable to change. That is what this play is all about, the need to break away from the past. As a Quebec Anglophone, I am now fully supportive of Quebec's right to self-determination. To think otherwise would only hold me back, making it impossible for me to move into the future. The only way forward is to put the dead in their graves where they belong. They are alive and in control of us as long as we believe in them and the system that honours their names.

BIBLIOGRAPHY

A History of Canadian Wealth. Gustavus Myers. James Lorimer & Co., 1975.

The Founding of Canada. Stanley B. Ryerson. Progress Books, 1975.

Unequal Union. Stanley B. Ryerson. Progress Books, 1975.

History of Quebec. Leandre Bergeron. N.C. Press, 1975.

Quebec: A History. Linteau/Durocher/Robert. James Lorimer & Co., 1983.

A Short History of Quebec. Young/Dickinson. Copp Clark Pittman Ltd., 1988.

The Private Capital. Sandra Gwyn. McClelland & Stewart, 1984.

We Walked Very Warily: A History of Women at McGill. M. Gillett. Eden Press, 1981.

McGill University. Stanley Brice Frost. Queen's University Press, 1984.

The National Dream. Pierre Berton. McClelland & Stewart, 1972.

The CPR: Century of Corporate Welfare. Robert Chodes. James Lorimer & Co., 1973.

Lords of the Line. Cruise/Griffiths. Viking Press, 1988.

Life and Times of Lord Strathcona. W.T.R. Preston. McClelland, Goodchild & Stewart, 1920.

My Generation of Politics and Politicians. W.T.R. Preston. D.A. Rose Publishing Co., 1927.

Ravenscrag: The Allan Royal Mail Line. Thomas E. Appleton. McClelland & Stewart, 1974.

Aequanimitas and Other Addresses. Sir William Osler. Blakiston Co., 1944.

Great Physician: A Short Life of Osler. Edith Reid. Oxford University Press, 1934

Rogues, Rebels and Geniuses: Story of Canadian Medicine. Donald Jack. Doubleday & Co., 1981.

Canada Under the Administration of the Earl of Dufferin. Geo. Stewart. Rose/Belford Co., 1878.

Helen's Tower: A Study of Lord Dufferin. Harold Nicolson. Constable & Co., 1937.

Life and Letters of Sir Wilfrid Laurier. Oscar Skeleton. McClelland & Stewart, 1965.

Georges Etienne Cartier, Montreal Bourgeois. Brian Young. McGill-Queen's Press, 1981.

Georges Etienne Cartier. Alistair Sweeny. McClelland & Stewart, 1976.

Trial of Thomas Neill Cream. W. Teignmouth Shore, ed. William Hodge & Co., 1923.

Victorian Studies in Scarlet. R.D. Altick. W.W. Norton & Co., 1970.

The Dark Angel: Aspects of Victorian Sexuality. F. Harrison. Fontana/Collins, 1977.

The Angel Makers: A Study in the Psychological Origins of Historic Change. G.R. Taylor. E.P. Dutton & Co., 1974.

Psychopathia Sexualis: A Reprint of the Original Published in 1894. Dr. Richard Von Krafft-Ebing. Paperback Library, 1965.

Hunting Humans: The Rise of Modern Multiple Murder. Elliot Leyton. McClelland & Stewart, 1986.

Murder for Profit. William Bolitho. Malboro Press, 1982.

Ravenscrag Rag

Raymond Filip

McGill Cakewalk

Untimely Life

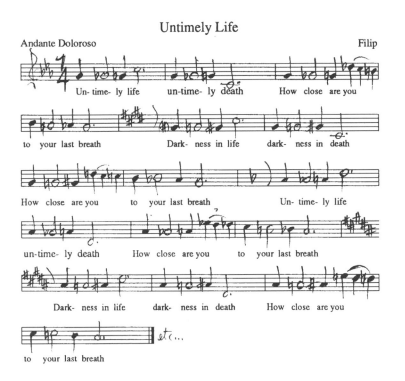

How low can you go?

A knock on the door but who is it for? you say to yourself it's some-bod-y else Please! no! Is it real-ly my time to
go say it's not so a sud-den quick moan with a cut to the bone
give me one min-ute more give me one min-ute more give me one min-ute more How low can you
go? How low can you go? How low can you go? you nev-er can
I want to kill some- one I want to kill some- one I want to kill some- one I want to kill someone I want to kill I want to kill I want to kill, kill, kill, kill, kill, kill,
kill, kill, kill, kill, kill, kill, kill, kill, kill, kill, kill, kill, kill, kill! long lone-ly kill!